Ruin has Sharp Fangs

M. R. Pritchard

Interior Art: Stockphotos from DepositPhotos. Elements, Filters, Fonts and digital manipulations with Canva.

Edited by: Kristy Ellsworth & Massiel Lago
Cover Design by: D'Arte Oriel

Midnight Ledger Publishing
14391 Spring Hill Dr. Suite 203
Spring Hill, FL 34609
MidnightLedger.com
First Edition February 2025
ISBNs: 9781957709864(Deluxe Edition),
9781957709871(Paperback)

About Ruin has Sharp Fangs by M. R. Pritchard

Ivy Calder never meant to bargain with Hell.

Drowning in debt and on the brink of losing her flower shop, Ivy signs what she thinks is a Valentine's delivery contract—only to discover she has summoned a Ledger Demon; a creature forged to enforce infernal law and collect what is owed.

Thorn is precise. Controlled. Lethal.

And bound by the contract, by the shop, and soon by Ivy herself.

As Valentine's Day approaches, Ivy and Thorn are forced into close proximity, long hours, and an intimacy neither of them anticipated. Thorn was never meant to want. Ivy was never meant to be collateral. But when desire crosses into blood and blood crosses into law, the Ledger takes notice.

Some systems are built to consume.

Some contracts are designed to ruin.

And some love stories bite back.

Ruin Has Sharp Fangs is a standalone dark fantasy romance featuring dangerous intimacy, morally gray choices, blood-bound devotion, and a love powerful enough to dismantle the laws of Hell itself.

Ruin Has Sharp Fangs expands the Veil of Shadows universe with a standalone novella set at the edge of Hell's authority.

When Ivy Calder accidentally summons a Ledger Demon while trying to save her flower shop, she becomes entangled with Thorn—an enforcer forged to collect souls and erase defiance.

But Thorn was created under laws that predate the current Queen of Hell. Laws that do not account for choice. Or love.

As Valentine's Day approaches and Hell tightens its claim, Ivy and Thorn form a bond that cannot be categorized, controlled, or collected. What begins as survival becomes rebellion.

This standalone novel features a cameo appearance by Remington, son of Meg, Queen of Hell, and explores the cost of dismantling ancient systems within the Veil of Shadows world.

No prior reading required.

CALDER FLORAL
TAKING VALENTINE'S DAY ORDERS!
Open
ESTABLISHED BY CHOICE.

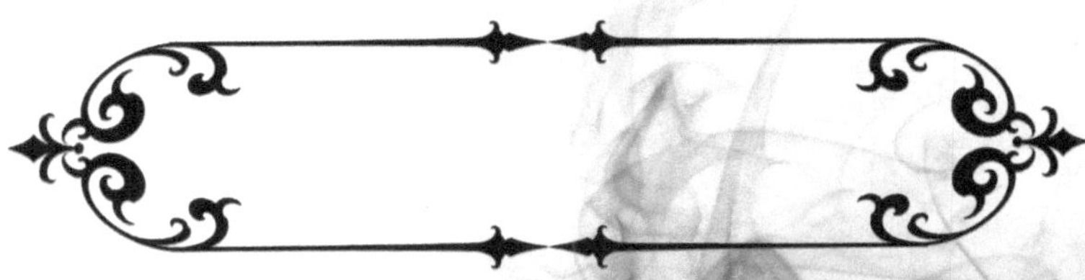

THE UNDERSIGNED OFFERS BINDING OF THEIR CORPOREAL SOUL, ENFORCEABLE UPON THE LEDGER'S JUDGEMENT.

THIS BOND IS IRREVERSIBLE.

I WANT YOU TO BELIEVE...TO BELIEVE IN THINGS YOU CANNOT.

BRAM STOKER. DRACULA

Chapter One

Pink wild roses, baby's breath, and eucalyptus were a special request. Ivy trimmed the stems and began wrapping green ribbon around them. A sharp sensation dragged across her finger and she looked down to see a thorn had gotten her. She hissed, grabbed a napkin and wrapped it around the cut.

"Great," she muttered. "I'll have to remake this." She pulled at the ribbon with her free hand and threw the blood stained ribbon away.

Outside, the streetlights on her little strip of downtown illuminated the sidewalk. Ivy looked up and focused on the glass display case, ribbon rack, the worktable where she'd spent the last eight years of her life, and the corner chair she never sat in because sitting meant thinking.

Ivy flipped the door sign to "Closed." She turned the deadbolt. Once. Twice. A third time because she didn't trust herself to remember doing it. It was a compulsion she hadn't been able to outgrow. It became worse when she was stressed. She'd find herself double and triple checking every-thing. Deadbolts, phone chargers, and more.

Valentine's week always did this to her.

It wasn't just the volume of orders; it was the way the phone rang like it was possessed, and how the online form pinged every time someone decided love required a hundred dollars' worth of imported roses and a handwritten apology. It was the pressure.

Every year, her accountant's voice lived in the back of her skull and whispered, *This is when you make it. This is the week you breathe again. You'll be in the green for months after this week.*

And as promised, every year Ivy made enough to keep the doors open.

She stepped behind the counter and picked up the stack of invoices. She had a headache and a tightness in her chest. She wished she had a cup of tea but these bills couldn't wait.

She spread the envelopes out like a tarot reading. Rent. Utilities. Wholesale supply. Credit card processing state-ment. A letter from the city that would either be a routine notice or the beginning of some fresh hell.

Her fingers were stained green from stems and ribbon dye. Little cuts along her knuckles had dried into thin red lines. The skin under her nails was raw. There was a rose thorn lodged under the pad of her thumb and she'd ignored it all day, because pain was like bills—if you paid attention to every single one, you wouldn't get anything done. Before bed she'd soak her hands and get the thorn out.

The overhead lights buzzed, one of them flickering like it wanted to give up on life. Ivy reached up and turned it off, leaving only the warm lamp by the register and the soft glow from the cooler in the back.

She exhaled.

"Okay," she told the empty shop. "Let's pretend I'm a person who has my life together."

The first envelope was rent. She didn't open it. She knew the total without looking. The second was electricity, and that one she did open, because hope was a stupid habit that never seemed to make the total lower. It wasn't. It never was.

Ivy set it down and kept going, each paper slice a thin, polite insult. After thirty minutes she stared at the sharp edge of her letter opener and wondered if a lobotomy could cure this.

She ignored that thought and kept going.

There was a late notice from a supplier who'd been patient for exactly one missed payment. Then came a credit card statement that might as well have been printed on a gravestone because that's how long she'd be paying it for. After that, she opened a reminder about her business insurance renewal. Perfect. Spectacular. She loved that for herself.

Lastly she came across a glossy flyer that said *CONGRATULATIONS!* as if she'd won something instead of being invited to apply for a loan with predatory interest and suspicious terms.

She rubbed her eyes until she saw stars. That lobotomy was sounding pretty good right now.

Valentine's Day was supposed to be the season where people spent money like it grew on trees. Roses, tulips, lilies, and anything red, pink, white, and drenched in love.

The problem was that Ivy's miracle was expensive and needed to be paid in advance.

Flowers arrived in bulk. Buckets needed water. The cooler ran nonstop. Ribbon came in giant spools and were cheapest when ordered in bulk. Boxes and tissue paper and delivery fuel and the stupid little plastic card picks shaped like hearts.

Her stomach growled loudly and she was reminded of the lack of groceries in her apartment. She couldn't buy any right now anyway.

In addition to the costs, there were the orders that didn't pay. The "my girlfriend will love this" bouquets that got disputed because the couple broke up before the delivery arrived. The last-minute cancellations. The corporate accounts that wanted invoices but took sixty days to pay. The guy who demanded a refund because the roses "didn't look like the website," as if Ivy could control nature. Wouldn't that be nice? If only she could control how the flowers grew, got cut, and how they were shipped to her.

Ivy pushed the letter opener out of her line of site. She reached the bottom of the stack and found an envelope that didn't match the rest.

Not just plain white with a printed label, this one was thick, creamy, like wedding invitation paper. The edges were clean. The flap was sealed with a small gold sticker in the shape of a heart, stamped with a design that looked like filigree... or maybe thorns, if you looked closely enough.

There was no return address.

The front read:

Ivy Calder
Calder Floral

The letters were embossed and it looked a little too fancy to be a bill, but she'd seen stranger things in her life.

For a moment, Ivy just stared. Her stomach sank the way it did when she saw a number too big, a deadline too close, an email from her landlord.

"Please be wholesale," she whispered. "A big, giant wholesale clearance." She closed her eyes for a moment and blessed herself. Then she slit it open with the edge of her fingernail. The paper that slid out was heavier than usual, the kind of cardstock used for fancy menus and life-altering decisions.

At the top, in elegant font that reminded her of a romantic horror novel cover, it said:

Settlement Notice

Ivy frowned. Settlement notice sounded official. But the bills were relentless and her brain was tired, and all day people had said things like. *Are you doing delivery on the 14th? Can I pay later? Can you just charge my card when it arrives?*

Maybe this was about a delivery service she'd used once and forgot to cancel. Maybe it was a billing change. Maybe it was a notice that the price of something had decreased for once.

She skimmed the letter. Numbers. Terms. Fine print. Her eyes snagged on a line that sounded vaguely familiar:

In exchange for relief from financial burden, the undersigned agrees to settlement—

Settlement. Great. Yes. She would love to settle. She would love relief. She would love to be done. What was this? It was sounding better already. She turned the paper sideways, looking for the amount due. There was a blank line with *Signature* printed beneath it.

Beneath that, another line labeled *Date*.

Ivy made an irritated sound.

Of course. Of course this was something she had to sign. Of course it couldn't be a simple invoice she could pay online in the morning. It had to be mailed. It had to be fancy. It had to be the kind of thing that punished her for not having a secretary. If she owed money, she was writing a check. Snail mail all the way baby. She was going to pay these people back in the slowest way possible.

Her phone buzzed on the counter. Another email notification. Another demand. Ivy didn't look at it.

She grabbed a pen from the cup by the register. It was one of the cheap black ones customers used to sign receipts and sometimes forgot to put back. The ink was halfway full at least. Perfect. Something pricked her fingertip where she'd held the pen. Not painful but more like the sharp warmth of a match head struck against a box. Ivy dropped the pen and flexed her hand before picking it back up noticing the thorn stuck in her thumbpad again.

"No regrets," she muttered to herself.

She leaned over the paper and signed in the space. *Ivy Calder.* She didn't notice the blood oozing down the pen. The second her pen lifted, she realized the ink looked strange. It didn't bleed into the paper like normal pen ink. It darkened looking deep, wet, and red.

Ivy stared at it, pen still hovering. A drop of blood splattered from the pen tip.

"Oh crap." Ivy reached for a napkin and wrapped it around her thumb.

She looked at the tip of the pen then back at the paper, confused.

"Okay," she said. "That's... weird."

She touched the signature with her finger and the ink was dry. No smear. No residue. And yet the red looked fresh, as if it had just been written.

She unwound the towel from her finger and picked at the tiny thorn stuck there, unable to get it out. It was like a sliver, but deep enough to draw blood when pressed on. She gave up, hoping her body would eventually expel it in a few days.

She scanned the page again, slower this time, looking for the company name. The sender. Something that might ring a bell. A tiny pulse of unease crawled up her spine.

The fine print seemed denser than it had a moment ago. She rubbed her eyes then blinked, and the words sharpened into clarity.

IN EXCHANGE FOR RELIEF FROM BURDENS OF THE business Calder Floral, the undersigned offers binding of their corporeal soul, enforceable upon the Ledger's judgement.

IVY'S MOUTH WENT DRY.

"What the hell?" she muttered. "Is this a wholesaler or a religious cult thing? I'm so confused."

Her pulse kicked hard once.

The smaller register lamp blinked twice and steadied. The cooler hummed, a little louder, like it was straining.

Ivy set the paper down and pressed her palm against the counter.

"Okay. I'm tired. This is what happens when you're tired. You read dramatic things on a bill and your brain turns it into mush."

The bell over the door rang. A clean, bright little chime. Just once. *Ding*.

Wait... that shouldn't happen, she'd locked the door, three times to be exact.

Ivy froze.

Her eyes went to the front windows. It was dark outside and the street was empty. A soft drift of something pale moved past the glass. She was sure it was either mist or the reflection of a passing car, though she hadn't heard any engine.

She forced herself to move, every nerve bristling. She stepped from behind the counter, silent on the worn hardwood floor, and stared at the door.

Nothing. No handle movement. No shadow. No figure outlined in the glass.

Her own reflection stared back at her. Dirty apron, messy hair, eyes too tired, and mouth set in a line. Her hair looked too red in the reflection and as she turned away, she tucked the loose pieces backup into her hair tie.

The bell rang again and this time, the door handle turned.

Ivy's throat tightened but she didn't scream. She didn't run. She didn't do anything heroic. She just stood there, unable to make her brain understand that doors weren't supposed to open when they were locked.

The deadbolt slid back with a sound like a blade being drawn and the door opened inward.

Cold air rolled into the shop. It carried a faint scent of woodsmoke and pine... and something else, something like iron and crushed roses. Blood?

A figure stepped inside. Tall. Broad-shouldered. Heavy boots *thunking* against the wood floor.

Ivy squinted. The streetlight didn't illuminate him correctly. Shadows clung to the edges of his coat, pooling at his feet like ink.

The door clicked shut but the bell didn't ring this time.

Ivy's heart hammered so hard her fingertips were throbbing. Her hand slid along the counter, fingers closing around the heavy glass vase she kept near the register for impulse buyers. Her first intention was to throw it, but the weight of it grounded her and calmed her racing thoughts.

"Can I help you?" she managed, voice steady through sheer disbelief. "The shop is closed."

The figure paused, mid step, then lifted his head. His eyes caught the light, and Ivy felt something in her stomach drop. She swallowed hard. He was darkness. His clothes, his eyes, his hair, and the way the shadows clung to him.

She suddenly wished she'd hidden a weapon behind the counter. Her fingers tightened around the vase. Maybe the vase would do? She used to play softball in college. She wasn't a pitcher but she was sure she could launch it across the shop and hit him square in the chest.

He smirked as he looked at her like she was a line on a

page. Like he'd found her. His gaze flicked briefly to the paper on the counter, then back to Ivy.

When he spoke, his voice was low and smooth in a way that didn't match the severity of his presence. It was carefully measured. He sounded like a businessman or a mafia man. She wasn't sure yet. But she couldn't stop staring.

"Ivy Calder," he said. He didn't ask. He didn't confirm. He stated it, like he already knew.

Ivy swallowed. "That's me." Shit, she hated that she revealed herself too quickly. She should have lied. What if he was a lawyer delivering a judgement for that credit card she stopped paying on last year?

The man stepped forward, the shadows moving with him like they were attached to his skin. The temperature in the shop dropped a few degrees. Ivy's breath started to fog in front of her mouth.

He stopped on the other side of the counter, close enough that Ivy could fully see him. She took in the edge of a dark collar, the gloves that looked too fine for a stranger in a small-town shop, and a faint pattern on his skin near his throat that looked like tattoos or lines like script–barely visible–as if something had been written beneath the surface. He was really tall, and though she hated to acknowledge it, he was really handsome. Like, magazine model kind of handsome.

His steady gaze remained on Ivy.

"Your signature has been recorded," he said.

Ivy blinked. "My what?"

He lifted his hand and set something on the counter. It was a second sheet of that same heavy paper. He slid it in front of her.

At the top, it read, *"Ledger Confirmation."*

Ivy's signature was already there in dark red script, like fresh blood.

Ivy's grip tightened around the vase again and the pad of her thumb throbbed.

"That's not mine." Her voice broke. She cleared her throat. "I signed a settlement notice. For... a bill. Or, I think it was some kind of religious grant for assistance. You know those rich churches do that sometimes. Charity. I was sure it was a charity offering to help. That's not my signature."

The man's expression didn't change, but something in the air shifted.

"There is no charity in Hell," he said, almost gently. "Only debts. Soul debts." His fingertips landed on the paper she'd signed just moments ago and he slid it next to the confirmation page he'd set down.

Ivy stared at him, her mind scrambling for normal explanations. Prank. Scam. Costume. Someone filming a TikTok in her shop. A fever dream. Was she high? Had she been drugged? She looked around, confused. Was this a dream or a nightmare?

The cold felt real and the smell of smoke seemed real. The paper at her fingertips bearing her signature surely felt real. She moved it closer and leaned in to get a better look.

Settlement Notice.

"What do you want?" Ivy demanded.

The man motioned to the paper on the counter and then at her.

His eyes were very dark–not black exactly–but the color of old ink. Of midnight. Of something that could swallow light and not be sorry about it.

"I am here," he said, "to collect."

Ivy's stomach turned over. "Collect what?"

His gaze held hers, steady and merciless.

The lamp by the register flickered once, as if it couldn't decide whether to keep lighting this scene.

"Your corporeal soul," he said.

Ivy's mouth opened but no sound came out.

You can't trade a soul for money. It wasn't flowers. It wasn't a late fee. Her corporeal soul was not for sale.

"The contract will activate soon," he continued.

Ivy stared at him, breath shallow. "What is this? I don't understand. How soon? Just erase my name!" She picked up the pen and tried to scribble out her signature but there was no ink. She gave up and slammed the pen down on the counter and took a deep breath.

"Who are you?" she whispered.

For the first time, something resembling interest touched his face. She could see it in an almost imperceptible tilt of his head.

"You may call me Thorn," he said. "It is the closest your tongue can manage."

Her grip on the vase trembled as she slid it closer to her.

"And what," Ivy said, forcing the words through her clenched teeth, "are you?"

Thorn's eyes didn't blink when he replied, "I am a Ledger Demon and you have summoned me."

Ivy looked at the paper. There was her signature. And the ink appeared too red to be regular ink. She glanced at the gold heart seal on the envelope, now dull in the lamp-light like it had never been gold at all, but something tarnished.

Then she looked back at him and her voice came out in a thin thread of disbelief, "Demons aren't real. This is a joke."

"You are mistaken." His voice was so calm.

"Well... whatever you think I did, I didn't mean to. I would like to politely decline your services. Please leave."

Thorn's gaze stayed on her, unmoved by intention. "Declination," he said, "does not alter enforcement."

Ivy's mind was spinning and it felt as if the walls had shifted closer. Ivy's heartbeat thundered.

Outside, the streetlight flickered.

Inside, the Ledger Confirmation paper on the counter pulsed faintly, like there was something alive beneath it trying to crawl out of the countertop.

Thorn's voice was quiet when he added, almost as if he were stating a weather report, "You are not afraid enough."

Ivy's fingers tightened around the vase until her knuckles went white and she realized she was holding it against her chest.

"Give me one reason," she said, voice shaking now despite her, "why I shouldn't call the police. The door was locked and you entered. I don't even know who or what you are. You are threatening me."

Thorn looked at her like she'd mentioned a minor inconvenience.

"You may call anyone you wish," he said. "The contract will still be there when they leave. The laws of your mortal realm do not apply to Hell."

Then his eyes dropped to the paper, and Ivy swore she saw the faintest movement beneath the ink, like a word rearranging itself. When he looked back up his voice didn't change, but the threat sharpened like a blade.

"And when time comes," Thorn said, "collection will begin."

The lamp flickered once more and Ivy realized with a sudden clarity that made her stomach plunge, something big had just happened. Something huge. Her landlord was going to be pissed because she was sure she just signed her name on a deed or something.

Ivy swallowed and set the vase down carefully on the counter.

CHAPTER TWO

Ivy woke up convinced she'd had a nightmare.

It wasn't even the cinematic kind with screaming and chasing but the exhausting, hyper-detailed kind. It was the kind that left residue on the brain; a bad dream stitched together from stress, caffeine, and the creeping dread of Valentine's week.

Demons. Contracts. Souls.

She lay in bed for a moment longer than usual, staring at the ceiling as pale winter light filtered through the skylight. The apartment above the shop was silent except for the hum of the radiator.

"Get moving, Ivy. No regrets. Get to work," she muttered to herself.

Ivy exhaled slowly and rolled out of bed.

The shower helped. Hot water washed away the lingering chill clinging to her skin. She dressed in familiar layers; a thermal shirt, sweater, and jeans already marked with faint green stains she'd never fully managed to scrub out. She twisted her long, red hair into a messy knot, grabbed her coat, and headed downstairs with the steady confidence of someone who had opened this shop hundreds of times before.

The bell over the door jingled as she unlocked it.

Cold air rushed in.

"Okay," Ivy murmured, flipping the sign to *Open*. "Let's do this."

She stepped behind the counter and froze.

The papers lay exactly where she'd left them.

Settlement Notice.

Crisp. Neat. Unmoved.

Her stomach dropped.

"Get it together," she muttered. "You were half asleep. You dreamed it. This is just weird scam mail."

Ivy glanced toward the front windows, half-expecting to see someone watching her from the sidewalk. Nothing. Just her reflection, pale and tense, staring back.

She reached out, fingers hovering for a second before closing around the stack. The paper was warm. She flinched and nearly dropped them.

"Nope," she whispered.

Ivy shoved the papers into the shelf beneath the counter behind a row of old receipt books and a dented tin of floral tape she had been saving.

Out of sight. Out of mind.

That's how this worked.

The bell jingled again.

"Ivy!" Evan's voice boomed cheerfully from the doorway. "Morning!"

She nearly jumped out of her skin.

"Jesus, Evan," she snapped, then pressed a hand to her chest. "Warn a person."

He laughed, stomping snow from his boots as he stepped inside. "If I warned you, I wouldn't get to see you startle so easily. You ready for hell week?"

She shot him a look. "Do not say that."

"Too late," he grinned. "I already did."

Evan leaned against the counter like he was at a bar, bright-eyed and irritatingly well-rested. He wore his usual delivery uniform and a knit cap pulled over his ears.

"I gassed up the van," he continued. "Checked the tires too. Weather report says light snow starting tonight, but nothing like last year."

Ivy winced. Last year had been a disaster. A sudden storm blew in and closed nearly all the main roads. Deliveries were delayed. Customers were furious. She'd slept on the shop floor for two nights straight processing the refunds and cried in the walk-in cooler where no one could hear her. Somehow, the store still stayed in the black that season.

"Light snow," she repeated. "That's what they said last year too. I fear this little town will never get it together."

Evan shrugged. "This time feels different. Roads should stay open. City's better prepared. The new mayor seems to be really organized." Evan thumbed toward the window. "He even pulled a few strings to get that fancy Italian restaurant, Bella Napoli, moved to a better location. People come all the way from New York City to eat there."

She hummed noncommittally and turned toward the worktable, pulling on her apron.

"So," Evan said, watching her closely. "You good? You look... tired."

"I'm always tired," Ivy replied automatically. "I had the strangest dream last night. Or... I think it was a dream."

He hesitated. "You look like you didn't sleep."

She tied the apron tighter than necessary. "I don't feel like I did."

Evan raised an eyebrow but let it go. "Well, orders are already stacking up. I've got three deliveries queued for today, nothing too crazy. Tomorrow's when it starts to get ugly."

"Of course it is," Ivy muttered.

She moved through the shop on autopilot and started with checking the coolers, topping off water levels, pulling fresh stems from buckets. The flowers were vibrant, healthy, and aggressively alive. Which was more than she could say for herself. Ivy paused, fingers brushing a rose petal.

"Hey," Evan said, breaking her concentration. "You got the Prescott order ready for later this week?"

"Yes," she replied quickly. "It's on the board."

He nodded. "Cool. Just checking. You know how they are."

She did. Prescott always complained. Always tipped badly. Always ordered last-minute.

At least some things still made sense.

Evan checked his clipboard. "Alright, I'm gonna start loading. Holler if you need me."

"Thanks," Ivy said.

He lingered a second longer. "You sure you're okay?"

She met his gaze and forced a smile. "I'm fine. Promise."

He nodded slowly. "I'll get you a coffee on my way back."

Ivy beamed. "You're my hero."

Evan smiled wide and tipped his hat. The bell above the door jingled as he headed back outside.

The shop settled into its familiar rhythm.

The phone rang twice. Two orders printed from the shop's website to the rhythmic sound of scissors snipping. Ivy lost herself in the work, grateful for the distraction.

But every so often, her gaze drifted back to the shelf behind the counter. The papers waited. A faint pressure began at the base of her skull. Maybe she should burn them?

"Not today," Ivy whispered under her breath as she wrapped a bouquet.

She had a shop to run. Flowers to sell. A week to survive.

Demons or dreams could wait.

Chapter Three

He was back in her locked shop looking like a damned supermodel from a gothic magazine. Ivy wanted to kick him out but she also wanted to stare at him a bit longer.

"You're going to have to explain this," she said. "Slowly. Preferably starting with why you're in my locked shop. I'm still not understanding what is happening right now." She rubbed her eyes. "Are you even real?"

Thorn didn't move.

He had just said he was a Demon, but he didn't have horns or fangs or claws—none of the thing's horror movies trained you to expect. He looked almost... restrained, like violence held behind glass. His coat hung straight, unwrinkled, the fabric so black it was swallowing light. The lines Ivy had noticed on his throat shifted subtly as he breathed, script sliding beneath skin.

He regarded her with the patience of a creature that did not need to rush. Ever.

"You invited me," he said.

"I did not."

"You signed." He gestured to the counter.

"I signed an invoice," she said. "I thought. It didn't say anything about Hell. I thought I was getting out of a debt."

Thorn's gaze flicked to her face, then back to the paper.

"Most do not read," he said. "That is why the Ledger persists. It is a mortal defect."

"The Ledger," Ivy repeated, voice tight. "That's what? A book?"

Something like approval brushed his expression, so subtle she might have imagined it.

"A record," Thorn said. "Of promises made and not kept. Of debts accrued. Of contracts sealed in blood."

"I didn't intend anything," Ivy snapped. "I was paying bills."

"You were seeking relief." His brows went up as if he were asking a question.

The word landed uncomfortably close to truth.

Ivy crossed her arms, nails biting into her sleeves. "So because I wanted my business to survive, I summoned a demon?"

"Yes."

She laughed, sharp and brittle. "That's ridiculous. You're not a demon. You're some bored handsome guy who is mistaking Valentine's Day week for Halloween."

Thorn's head tipped to the side. "Handsome?"

"Forget I said that." Ivy waved her hand.

Thorn's eyes lifted to hers again. There was no humor in them. No irritation. But, there was a spec of amusement before it disappeared in a second, replaced by darkness.

"You desired release from burden," he said. "You signed

a settlement notice due at the end of the week. The Ledger answered accordingly."

Ivy's laugh died in her throat.

"Valentine's week?" she echoed.

Thorn inclined his head a fraction. "The season in which devotion is the strongest. You are devoted to this..." he looked around as though he were just realizing where he was. "You are devoted to this flower shop."

Something cold slid down her spine.

"You mean love," she said. "I love my flower shop. It is my life."

"I mean binding," Thorn replied. "You are bound to it by mortal means."

"I am bound by bills. But yes, I love this shop." Ivy rubbed at her temples. She could feel a headache blooming, tight and insistent. This was stress. Exhaustion. A hallucination brought on by caffeine and fear and too many twelve-hour days. That was the only real answer to all of this.

"Okay," she said slowly. "Let's pretend for a second that you're real. That Hell is real. That contracts like this exist." She tapped the paper with one finger. "What exactly do you think you're collecting from me?"

Thorn didn't answer immediately. His gaze drifted around the shop, taking in details Ivy hadn't realized were visible from where he stood; the handwritten chalkboard sign by the door advertising *Valentine's Day Specials*, the faded Polaroid taped near the register of her younger self on opening day, and the small vase of dried baby's breath she kept because it reminded her of her mother.

The shadows at his feet shifted as his attention moved.

"Your soul," he said again. "Ivy Calder, you are talking in circles. It is frustrating me. This is the third time you've asked."

"I live my life in clusters of three. It's a compulsion, I can't help it." Ivy exhaled hard. "And a soul is not a thing you can invoice."

"It is a thing you offered."

"I didn't offer that," she said, heat rising in her chest. "I offered money. Or settlement."

Thorn looked at her then, and she felt the full weight of his attention settle on her skin. It wasn't invasive. It was clinical. Like she was being assessed for structural integrity.

She suddenly regretted her thoughts of wanting a lobotomy.

"The contract does not require money," he said. "It requires your soul."

Ivy's mouth went dry. She stopped, a chill crawling through her words. "People don't just give that away."

"People give it away constantly," Thorn said. "They simply do not realize it is being taken. It happens more often than you think."

The cooler hummed louder, the sound grating in Ivy's ears.

She shook her head. "No. I'm sorry. You've got the wrong person. I'm not losing my soul."

"Not yet," Thorn said.

The words were quiet. Certain.

Ivy's heart thudded against her ribs.

"Listen," she said, forcing herself to breathe. "If this is some kind of a mistake, then there has to be a way to undo it. Void it. Cancel it. I cancel."

She lifted the paper and tore it cleanly in half. For a second, nothing happened. Then it seemed as though something slammed into Thorn. He hissed and staggered back a step, one hand bracing against the counter. The shadows surged upward. The torn halves of the contract flared white-hot in Ivy's hands, heat biting her palms until she dropped them with a cry.

They hit the counter and fused back together. The ink of Ivy's signature pulsed once, bright and wet.

Ivy stared.

Thorn straightened slowly, breath controlled, jaw tight. The script beneath his skin flared brighter, lines of red threading up his throat and disappearing beneath his collar.

"That," he said evenly, "was unwise."

Ivy swallowed. "What was that?"

Thorn looked down at the paper, then back at her. Something had changed in his expression. He looked like he was calculating something, thinking.

"The contract is malformed now," he said.

Ivy's pulse spiked. "Malformed?"

"It bound improperly." His gaze sharpened.

"I don't know what that means. You talk weird."

"It means," Thorn said, voice low between gritted teeth, "that the binding reached for the nearest eligible anchor." The words under his skin were rearranging, rewriting across his neck and arms.

"Which was...?" she asked. Unease settling through her as she recalled the way he'd hissed just a few moments ago as though he were in pain.

Thorn's eyes darkened, ink swallowing iris. "Me."

Uh oh.

"No," Ivy said immediately. "No, that's not possible. This is nuts." Her heart hammered so loudly she was sure he could hear it. She could hear it. "What happens now?" she demanded.

Thorn glanced toward the door. "I cannot leave," he said. "The contract tethers me to the point of summoning."

"My shop," Ivy whispered.

"Yes."

"So," she said, staring at the glowing paper. "Let me get this straight. I accidentally summoned a Ledger Demon and I bound him to my flower shop. And now... what? We wait?"

Thorn inclined his head. "Until dawn," he said. "And then we will see what the contract demands."

Ivy dragged a hand down her face. "This is the worst Valentine's week I've ever had," she muttered. "I thought these bills were bad but this really takes the cake."

For the first time since he'd arrived, Thorn hesitated. It was subtle, just a fraction of a second too long before he spoke but Ivy recognized it.

"Statistically," he said, "most summoners consider their experience transformative."

She snorted. "That's one word for it."

Silence stretched between them.

Outside a car passed, headlights sliding across the windows. Thorn's shadow didn't move with the light. It stayed fixed, anchored, like it belonged to the floor.

Ivy looked up at him.

"You're really stuck here," she said quietly.

"Yes."

"And you won't hurt me?"

"I cannot," Thorn said. "Not unless the contract permits it."

"I didn't agree to being hurt. Does it?"

His gaze dropped briefly to her hands, then returned to her face.

"No," he said.

Something inside Ivy loosened with relief.

"Okay," she said, exhaling. "Then you can stand there and be terrifying, but you're not touching anything. And you're definitely not touching me."

Thorn's mouth curved into a small smile of acknowledgment. "As you wish," he said.

She rubbed her head and pulled the scrunchie out that was holding up all of her long red hair. "You are giving me a migraine. I just... I need to think for a moment." She rested her face in her hands and closed her eyes.

Chapter Four

Ivy blinked slow and long. When she opened her eyes again, she was still on the stool behind the counter. Her neck ached. Her hands were numb. The shop was dim.

And Thorn was still there. He was now near the front windows, shoulders squared, gaze angled toward the door as if he were listening for something she couldn't hear.

It wasn't a dream.

"You don't sleep," Ivy said hoarsely.

Thorn's head turned slightly. "No."

"Do you get tired?"

"No."

"Lucky you," she muttered, rubbing her face.

Thorn's eyes flicked to the window, where the sky was just beginning to lighten from pitch to charcoal.

She stood, joints protesting, and circled the counter.

Thorn watched her every step.

"Okay," she said, stopping a few feet from him. "Let's get this over with. You said you were here to collect. Try taking my soul. Let's get this over with, I need to get to work soon."

Thorn turned fully toward her. The shadows at his feet shifted, spreading slightly across the floor like spilled ink. The air grew cold enough to sting Ivy's nose.

"Stand still," he said.

She lifted her chin. "I am standing still."

He stepped closer.

Every instinct Ivy had was screaming at her to run, but she forced herself to stay rooted, nails biting into her palms. He smelled nice, like pine forests and apples.

Thorn lifted his gloved hand but he didn't touch her. The space between his fingers and her chest was barely an inch and it burned.

His face twisted and Thorn staggered back with a sharp fractured inhale. The shadows recoiled violently, snapping back toward him as if yanked by a leash.

Ivy cried out, lunging forward without thinking, trying to stop him from falling. The moment her fingers brushed his sleeve, a shock tore through her arm. Heat. Fire. A brutal, echoing pulse slammed into her heart and bounced back.

She screamed.

Thorn roared.

The sound was not human. It shook the shelves, sent petals fluttering loose from arrangements, and rattled the windows in their frames.

Ivy was thrown backward, landing hard on the floor. Pain flared up her spine, but she barely felt it over the pounding in her chest.

The Ledger Confirmation page on the counter flared bright white.

Thorn dropped to one knee, head bowed, one hand braced against the floor. The script beneath his skin blazed, lines crawling up his neck and disappearing beneath his hairline.

For a terrible second, Ivy thought she'd killed him.

"Thorn," she gasped, scrambling to her feet.

He lifted his head slowly, breath controlled but ragged at the edges. "Do not," he said tightly, "touch me."

Her hands hovered uselessly in the air. "You're the one who tried to touch me."

"I did not," he snapped and then gently said, "I did not make contact."

"Then why did it hurt you?"

He pushed himself upright, jaw clenching, movements stiff like a robot recalibrating after damage.

"The contract," he said. "It forbids collection."

Ivy stared at him. "You mean it stopped you."

"Yes."

"And me?" Her stomach flipped. "So I can't touch you either."

"Not until something changes."

"Great," she muttered. "That's just... fantastic." She glanced from the corner of her eye at him. "I didn't want to touch you anyway. I just thought you were going to fall earlier and I didn't want you to break anything."

She didn't want to touch him, didn't really see touching him in her future. She really just wanted this whole escapade to end.

The silence that followed was thick and uneasy. He was watching her under dark, hooded eyes.

Ivy looked at the counter and at the paper glowing faintly beneath the lamp. She finally let out a shaky breath. "So what happens now?"

Thorn's gaze drifted again to the windows.

"The contract seeks resolution," he said. "Until then, I am tethered."

She gestured helplessly around them. "So you're... what? A very scary employee?"

He shrugged. "I don't work for you, but I can't leave. My soul is bound to Hell."

"And if it doesn't resolve?"

His eyes darkened. "Then it will escalate."

Ivy's stomach dropped. "Escalate how?"

"The Ledger will attempt to correct the imbalance," Thorn said. "By force, if necessary."

Her pulse spiked. "Force against who?"

"Against me," he said. "Or against you."

"Mother of pearl," Ivy swore softly.

She dragged a hand through her hair and paced, boots scuffing the floor as she walked away. She ended up back behind the counter, and he slowly followed and stopped across from her.

"You said the soul collection can be fulfilled or denied," she said. "What does denial look like?"

Thorn didn't answer immediately.

"That bad, huh?" she pressed.

"It requires authorization from the throne of Hell," he said finally. "You can attempt refusal."

"I can refuse," Ivy said quickly. "I'm very good at that."

His gaze sharpened. "Are you?"

Ivy stopped pacing. "Yes."

"Then you must do so without contradiction," Thorn said. "The throne of Hell does not take lightly to liars."

Her throat tightened. "That's... vague."

"Some lie about their life in an attempt to keep their souls intact."

Ivy laughed, sharp and humorless. "You don't know my life."

"Then tell me," Thorn said.

The words landed heavily between them.

Ivy opened her mouth, then shut it. Her gaze slid away, toward the shop—toward the half-finished bouquets, the delivery list taped to the cooler, and the small handwritten sign near the register that read *Thank you for supporting local*.

"I built this place by myself," she said quietly. "I don't have anyone to lean on. I don't have time to fall apart. If that's what your contract needs, then great. It picked the wrong person."

Thorn watched her, expression unreadable.

"You are exhausted," he said.

"So?"

"So exhaustion breeds desire for relief," he replied. "Which is how you summoned me."

Ivy's jaw tightened. "I didn't realize I was summoning a demon."

"I am aware."

The honesty of it startled her.

"Good," she said. "Then this should be easy."

Thorn's gaze lingered on her face a moment longer than necessary.

"Ease," he said, "is not a factor the Ledger recognizes."

Ivy hugged herself, suddenly cold. "You said you can't leave."

"Correct."

"And you can't touch anything?"

"Only what is permitted."

"What's permitted?"

Thorn looked around the shop again.

"The collateral."

Ivy's breath caught. "The shop?"

The Ledger Confirmation page slid across the counter on its own, stopping neatly between them.

At the bottom, new text slowly bled into being, *Collateral Designation: Place of Summoning.*

Ivy stared at it. "My shop."

"Yes."

"So you can protect it."

"Yes."

"And harm anyone who threatens it. Like... bill collectors?"

"Yes."

A thought sparked—terrifying and strangely comforting. Well, for the first time ever she wouldn't be running this place alone for the Valentine's Day holiday. But after the holiday... would she keep her soul?

"And me?" she asked quietly.

Thorn's gaze lifted to hers.

"You are not collateral," he said. "You are the contract holder."

Something warm twisted in her chest, but she ignored it. "Meaning?" she pressed.

His voice was low when he answered. "Meaning I am bound to ensure your survival until resolution."

Ivy swallowed. "Well," she said faintly, "that's... something."

The first ray of sunlight slipped through the front window, pale and tentative.

The Ledger page pulsed once.

Thorn straightened, every line of him going taut.

"The reckoning begins," he said.

Ivy's heart kicked painfully.

"And what does that mean?" she whispered.

Thorn looked at her, eyes dark and intent.

"It means," he said, "the contract is now watching."

CHAPTER FIVE

BY THE TIME THE FIRST DELIVERY DRIVER texted *On my way*, Ivy had accepted two things she didn't want to admit to.

One: Thorn was not leaving.

Two: She still had to make bouquets.

The shop looked normal in daylight—almost insultingly so. Sunlight softened the edges of the ribbon rack and warmed the wood floor. The front windows glittered with frost. The cooler hummed like it always did. If Ivy ignored the blood-ink paper on the counter and the tall, shadowed figure who did not belong in any of her ordinary mornings, she could pretend she'd simply pulled an all-nighter again.

She couldn't.

Thorn stood near the front window, facing outward as if he were posted there, an unmoving statue in the corner of her vision. The shadows at his feet didn't stretch the way shadows should. They pooled and held, dark ink on the floor.

Ivy dragged her apron on and tied it with sluggish fingers.

"Okay," she said, mostly to herself. "We're doing this. Somehow."

Thorn's head turned slightly. "You are proceeding?"

"Yeah," Ivy muttered. "That's what happens when you own a small business. Even Hell doesn't get you a day off. Or demons. Or weird contracts that arrive in the middle of the night."

His gaze flicked over the shop, measuring. "You continue despite danger."

"I continue despite everything." Ivy grabbed a bucket of fresh stems and set it on the worktable. Her arms felt like lead. "If I stop, it all collapses. I must persist." The last words slipped out with a fake accent that sounded British.

Something in the air shifted.

The roses in the bucket closest to Thorn leaned, stems angling subtly toward him as if pulled by a tide. Ivy stopped mid-motion, watching them.

"That's... not normal," she said.

Thorn's eyes followed the movement, then returned to Ivy.

"Collateral responds," he said.

"Collateral?" Ivy echoed, irritation flaring. "My flowers are not collateral. They're inventory. They're... hell, they're flowers."

"In Hell," Thorn said, "ownership is a form of claim. Claim is a form of binding."

Ivy made a face. "You make everything sound like a prison."

"It is, in the end," Thorn replied, as if she'd stated a weather fact.

Ivy stared at him. "Do you ever... lighten up?"

Thorn blinked once. "No."

"Good to know."

Her phone buzzed again. Another order. Another reminder that Valentine's Day was barreling toward her like a truck.

She sighed and got to work.

The first bouquet was classic: red roses, baby's breath, eucalyptus. She stripped thorns, cut stems, wrapped ribbon. She kept glancing up, and every time she did, Thorn was watching and every so often his gaze dipped to her hands with something that felt almost... curious.

The bell over the door jingled, and Ivy flinched before she could stop herself.

A woman stepped inside with a travel mug and a cranberry colored scarf. Normalcy breathed warmth into the shop.

"Morning!" the woman chirped. "Oh, it smells incredible in here. I love the smell of roses."

Ivy forced a smile and tried to relax. "Morning. What can I get you?"

The woman's gaze drifted past Ivy, snagging on Thorn near the window.

Her steps slowed and her smile faltered, not entirely disappearing but... tightening, like her face didn't trust what it was seeing.

"Oh," she said, voice dipping. "he scared me. I didn't see anyone through the window."

Ivy's throat went dry. "Can I help you find something or are you just looking?"

The woman kept glancing at Thorn as if he were a large dog that might bite if she moved wrong. Ivy watched confusion ripple across her expression.

"Is he... with you?" the woman asked, lowering her voice as if Thorn couldn't hear. "Do you need help?" The woman slipped a phone out of her bag and dialed 9-1-1, her finger hovering over the *call* button.

Thorn's gaze slid to the woman, and the temperature in the room dropped so sharply Ivy felt it against her neck.

The woman shivered.

"No." Ivy cleared her throat loudly. "He's—uh. Security."

Thorn's head tilted a fraction, and a smirk crossed his face.

Security.

The woman nodded too fast. "Smart. Yeah. I mean, people get wild this week."

"Exactly," Ivy said, leaning hard into the lie. "People can get very passionate about flowers. And deliveries."

The woman laughed a little too loudly and moved to the display case, choosing a small arrangement from the shelf near the register.

"I love these," Ivy said, pointing out the Calla Lilies. "This is a special color for the holiday. The flower farm developed this color of peony. Can't find it anywhere else." She repositioned the pure white bloom with a violet center.

"It's just beautiful," the woman agreed. "It will look lovely on my desk."

As Ivy rang her up, the woman's fingers fumbled with her card. Her cheeks had gone pale.

"Have a great day," Ivy said brightly.

"You too," the woman whispered, and nearly sprinted out.

The bell jingled and silence fell.

Ivy exhaled slowly and pressed her hands to the counter.

"You did something," she accused.

"I stood," Thorn said.

"She looked like she saw a ghost."

"She saw a predator," Thorn corrected, calm as ever. "Her body recognized it. I am a demon."

Ivy swallowed. "Can you stop being that way? You don't look like a demon you just look angry."

Thorn's gaze lifted to the ceiling, as if considering the structure of reality. "No."

"Cool." Ivy grabbed the next order slip. "This is going to be a great week."

The day kept coming at her in small waves. Customers trickled in; some were cheerful, some frantic, some guilty.

And every single one of them reacted to Thorn. Not overtly. Not dramatically. But in the subtle ways Ivy understood all too well from years of reading people: a hesitation at the threshold, a shift in posture, a laugh that didn't land, eyes avoiding the corner he stood in while being unable to stop darting back.

One man walked in, spotted Thorn, and immediately said, "Actually—wrong shop," before backing out.

A teenage boy tried to flirt with Ivy while ordering

roses, then went quiet mid-sentence when Thorn's gaze flicked toward him.

A woman buying a bouquet for her sister muttered, "You've got... intense vibes," and laughed as if it was a compliment. Her hands shook while she paid. "Is he single?"

Ivy shrugged.

By late afternoon, Ivy's body was running on fumes and spite. The delivery drivers came and went with boxes and buckets. She tied bows with fingers that felt detached from her brain. She kept swallowing yawns and pretending the bruise-dark circles under her eyes were just "busy season."

She told herself she could do this.

She told herself she had no choice, no regrets.

When the last customer finally left and the bell stilled again, Ivy locked the door, flipped the sign to CLOSED, and leaned her forehead against the glass for one quiet second embracing the coolness on her face.

Then she turned. Thorn was still there. As if time didn't exist for him.

"As thrilling as this has been," Ivy said, voice rasping, "I'm going upstairs."

Thorn's gaze followed her. "You will sleep."

"God, I hope so." She waved her hand. "After whatever weirdness happened here last night and not getting even a wink of sleep, I'm exhausted."

He said nothing, which Ivy took as agreement.

She grabbed her keys from the hook under the counter and moved toward the narrow staircase tucked behind the cooler. The apartment above the shop was small; just a one bedroom, one bath, a kitchenette she barely used, and a skylight that leaked when it rained.

It was cheap, it was close, and it was home.

She paused at the bottom step and looked back at him, suddenly aware of the absurdity of what she was about to do.

Leave a Ledger Demon alone in her shop.

"Okay," Ivy said, planting her hands on her hips. "Ground rules."

Thorn's head tilted. "Proceed."

"Number one," Ivy began, counting on her fingers like she was addressing a problematic employee. "Do not murder me while I sleep."

"I cannot," Thorn said immediately.

"Okay," Ivy said, "comforting. But I'm still saying it out loud. Number two: don't damage the shop."

His gaze slid to the shelves, the worktable, the cooler. "It is collateral."

"So you won't."

"I will not," Thorn said.

Ivy narrowed her eyes. "Number three: don't rob me."

Thorn blinked once. "Rob you?"

"Yes. Like... steal stuff."

"I do not require your currency," Thorn said. "Only your contract. Your soul."

"Right," Ivy muttered. "Not creepy at all. Still. No stealing."

Thorn's expression remained unreadable, but something about the stillness of his mouth suggested he found the concept... strange.

"I will not," he said.

Ivy hesitated then added, because her exhaustion had stripped away her filter, "And number four: don't eat my customers."

Thorn's gaze flicked to her face and, for the first time since he'd arrived, something in his eyes shifted—an unfamiliar pause, as if he needed to decide whether she was joking.

"I do not eat... customers or humans of any kind," he said finally.

Ivy's mouth twitched. "You really are the fun kind of demon."

"I am not just a demon," Thorn corrected.

"Ledger Demon," she said. "Right. Excuse me. Paperwork demon."

His jaw tightened faintly. "Do not reduce my classification."

Ivy smiled despite herself, the first real one she'd managed all day. "Do you want me to use your full title? Ledger Demon of Hell, Enforcer of Fine Print?"

Thorn's gaze sharpened, but she could feel an edge of discomfort radiating off him, like she'd stepped too close to something human in him. Or what was once human in him.

"I enforce," he said simply.

"Mm." Ivy took one step up, then stopped and looked down at him from the stair. "You're going to give me your word, right? That you won't do any of those things."

Thorn's gaze locked onto hers. "You already have it," he said.

A beat passed. Ivy's stomach fluttered in a way she refused to examine.

"Good," she said, too briskly. "Because I'm exhausted and if I wake up and my shop is on fire, I will—"

"You will what?" Thorn asked, quiet.

Ivy blinked. "I don't know."

Thorn's eyes darkened and she was suddenly aware that he was kind of intimidating, and tall, and dark and... he was decent-looking with dark wavy hair and a sharp jawline. He could pass for security, just not in that outfit.

She climbed two more steps then paused again, her exhaustion making her reckless.

"Do you have somewhere you're supposed to be?" she asked, voice softer now. "Like... do you have a home? A family? A wife?"

Thorn didn't answer immediately. Instead, his gaze lowered.

"No," he said at last.

Ivy's throat tightened unexpectedly. "No?"

He shook his head once; a small, final motion. "I have no one. I am without family."

The words were flat, factual. But the emptiness behind them wasn't.

"I am a Ledger Demon," he added, as if that explained everything. "I exist only for enforcement."

Ivy stared down at him, her chest doing something unpleasantly tender.

"That's bleak," she murmured.

"It is accurate," Thorn replied.

Ivy swallowed. Her fingers tightened around her keys. She forced a shrug into her shoulders like she could shake off the feeling.

"Well," she said, attempting lightness, "try not to miss me too much while I'm upstairs."

Thorn's gaze lifted to her face again, dark and steady. "I do not miss," he said.

Ivy's smile turned crooked. "That might be a lie. You might grow to miss me."

"It is nothing I'd lie about," Thorn replied.

"Then," Ivy said, voice tipping into something dangerously close to flirting, "that means you're going to stand there all night thinking about me."

Thorn's posture went very still, as if her words had triggered some internal warning.

His eyes narrowed slightly.

"I will stand here," he said, carefully. "Because I am tethered. Because *you* tried to rip up the agreement."

Ivy bit the inside of her cheek to keep from saying anything else. As odd as this entire situation was, he was stuck there because of her. She didn't know what she was doing, but it was still her fault.

She climbed the rest of the stairs, reached the small landing, and turned back to look down at him.

Thorn had moved and now stood at the foot of the stairs like a sentinel. He looked up at her then turned and stood with his back to the stairs like a guard dog.

For a second, Ivy wondered what it had cost him to have no one, to exist only as a function.

She didn't know why she cared. She didn't have the energy to care. Still, she could treat him kindly–it was in her nature.

"Goodnight, Thorn," she said quietly. "I'm sorry I trapped you here."

He didn't respond at first.

Then, as Ivy unlocked the apartment door she heard his voice from below, strangely intimate in the stillness.

"Sleep, Ivy Calder," Thorn said. "You will need strength for the week ahead."

Ivy paused with her hand on the knob.

"Yeah," she whispered, mostly to herself. "I bet."

She stepped inside, locked the door, and leaned against it for a moment, exhaling a heavy breath. Ivy realized that for the first time in years that she wasn't alone in the building, which should have terrified her. Instead, exhaustion dragged her under and as she crossed the apartment toward her bed, she caught herself thinking one ridiculous impossible thought: *At least he gave his word.*

And in a world where everything could fall apart with one missed payment, a promise felt like the rarest thing she'd ever been handed.

Chapter Six

Ivy walked down the stairs with a coffee cup in each hand. She felt compelled to bring Thorn something hot to drink and test his disclaimer of not eating anything. Also, she felt guilty that she'd forced him to sleep in the shop with no comfortable furniture or a blanket. It was rude of her.

She found him near the window.

"Did you sleep?" she asked.

He didn't look away, simply watched all of the people trudging by in the snow.

"I don't sleep," Thorn reminded her.

"That's right." She moved closer. "I brought you coffee."

He looked at the mug in her hand then slowly accepted it. He smelled the liquid.

Ivy took a sip. "I wasn't sure what you'd like so I made it like mine with milk and honey."

"Milk and honey," he muttered into the cup before taking a sip.

Ivy watched. "I thought you didn't eat?"

"I don't, doesn't mean I cannot."

Ivy made a face and turned away. "You're impossible."

They stood side by side while they people-watched. After a few minutes, Ivy realized Thorn had changed his clothing. He was no longer wearing a long coat and a suit like the night he'd arrived. He was wearing black cargo pants, a black shirt and a vest that said *Security* across the front.

"You changed your clothes?" Ivy asked.

"It appeared I was making your customers nervous. Does this fit your lie of me being security?"

Ivy nodded. "I don't think it was your clothing that was off-putting."

"What was it?"

"Probably your demeanor."

"I am a Ledger Demon."

"You don't look like a demon. I don't see horns or scaled skin or fangs."

He smiled, flashing his teeth and Ivy noticed the sharp fangs set back in his jaw.

"Oh..." She took a few steps back. "Pardon me," she replied in exaggeration but couldn't stop looking at him.

"You're staring."

"Sorry." She turned and sipped at her coffee. "I don't know what's wrong with me. One minute I'm living life, the next I'm talking to a demon. This is nuts." She took another sip. "When you say you don't eat, is that because you drink blood or something?"

Thorn's lips rose in a half-smile and he glanced at her neck.

Ivy couldn't control the flush that shifted over her skin. She held up a finger. "Slow down, cowboy."

"I am not a cowboy."

"Don't bite my customers."

"I won't."

Ivy sighed and walked to the counter, reaching for the ribbon spool.

She worked in silence for a few minutes, the familiar rhythm settling her—strip thorns, cut, arrange, wrap. The scent of flowers layered thickly in the air, rose and eucalyptus, freesia and green leaves, a hint of soil clinging stubbornly to the stems. She was halfway through a dozen roses when she realized Thorn had moved.

He was closer and stood at the worktable, a careful distance away, hands clasped behind his back.

"You're hovering," Ivy said without looking up.

"I am observing."

"Uh-huh." She snipped a stem. "You can observe from over there."

"I am permitted to assist."

Her hands stilled. She looked up slowly. "Assist how?"

Thorn's gaze flicked to the pile of delivery boxes, the ribbon scraps, the stack of order slips threatening to topple. "By reducing strain."

Ivy studied him, suspicion warring with fatigue. "Have you ever arranged flowers?"

"No."

"I can't imagine a Ledger Demon would."

"Never."

"Then how exactly do you plan to help?"

"I can organize," Thorn said. "Carry. Cut ribbon. Record orders."

Her brow creased. "You... can use scissors?" She held up the scissors and snipped the air; the scissors made a metallic, pleasant sound.

He paused. "Yes. I am not an invalid."

Ivy stared at him for a long moment, then laughed. "Okay. You can cut ribbon."

She handed him the spool and a pair of scissors before she could talk herself out of it.

He took them carefully, like objects that might explode.

"Short strips," she instructed. "For the hand-tied bouquets."

Thorn nodded once and set to work. He was precise. Each ribbon strip was identical in length, cut cleanly, edges perfectly straight. He stacked them in neat rows on the counter, alignment exact enough to make Ivy's chest ache.

"Wow," she murmured. "You're... unsettlingly good at that."

"I enforce uniformity," Thorn replied. "But I typically use a different style of weapon to cut."

"That tracks." She took a step away from him. "Scissors are not a weapon, by the way."

They worked side by side but not touching, moving around each other in a careful dance that never quite closed the distance. Ivy arranged flowers. Thorn prepared supplies. The shop felt calmer, as if something about his presence steadied the day instead of amplifying it.

From the corner of her eye, Ivy noticed a subtle lean, a tilt of petals. Roses angled toward Thorn as he passed, heads lifting like they recognized him. Leaves rustled softly without breeze.

"Okay," Ivy said finally, pointing with her clippers. "Explain that."

Thorn followed her gesture. His expression tightened. "Collateral responds to authority."

"They're *flowers*," Ivy said. "They don't respond to authority. They respond to water and sunlight."

"And binding," Thorn said.

She shook her head, half-amused, half-unsettled. "You're not touching them."

"No."

"You're not breathing on them."

"No."

"Then why do they lean toward you like they want your autograph?"

Thorn's gaze lingered on the roses, something unreadable passing through his eyes. "They recognize the Ledger."

"That's ominous."

"It is accurate."

Ivy rolled her eyes and went back to work, but her pulse had picked up. She didn't miss the way Thorn's gaze followed her hands, tracked the small movements, the sure cuts, the way she coaxed beauty from flowers.

After an hour, Ivy's wrists screamed. She set the clippers down with a groan and flexed her fingers. The sliver lodged in her thumb ached. She picked at it, trying to get it out.

"I need a break," she declared. "I'm getting water." She turned toward the sink, then stopped.

Thorn was staring at his hand. The script beneath his

skin glowed brighter than usual, lines burning red against the pale darkness of him. The light pulsed then flared. Thorn hissed quietly.

Ivy was at his side in an instant. "What happened?"

He tried to pull his hand back, but she caught his wrist without thinking.

Pain snapped through her palm, like touching a stovetop that had just been turned off. She sucked in a breath and released him, heart hammering.

"Sorry," she said automatically. "I forgot."

"You should not touch me," Thorn said, jaw tight. "The Ledger—"

"I know," Ivy snapped, already reaching for the first aid kit under the counter. "Sit."

"I'm fine."

"Sit," she repeated, and to her own surprise, her voice carried the same tone she used with panicking grooms and overbearing mothers-of-the-bride.

Thorn hesitated. Then he sat.

The stool creaked under his weight. Ivy knelt in front of him, ignoring the way her knees protested, and took his hand again—carefully this time, just enough contact to work.

The heat was worse up close. The script along his skin glowed angrily, lines raised like fresh scars.

"The Ledger burned you," she murmured.

"It corrected an inefficiency," Thorn said. "I exceeded assistance parameters."

"By cutting ribbon?"

"By wanting to continue," he said.

The word landed like a dropped glass.

Ivy stilled. "Wanting."

He looked away.

She grabbed antiseptic and gauze, movements automatic. "You're allowed to want things."

"No," Thorn said quietly. "Ledger Demons are not."

She frowned, cleaning the edge of the burn where the glow had faded to a raw, angry red. "That doesn't make sense."

"It makes perfect sense," Thorn replied. "Want creates bias. Bias compromises enforcement."

"Then how do you do anything?" Ivy asked softly. "How do you exist without wanting?"

Thorn's jaw worked. "By function."

Ivy wrapped the gauze around his hand, fingers brushing his skin with deliberate care. The heat lessened, as if the act itself soothed the burn.

"Function sounds lonely," she said.

"I do not experience loneliness," Thorn replied.

She tied the bandage and looked up at him. "That sounds like something you were told."

His gaze snapped to hers.

For a moment, the shop felt too small.

"I was created to enforce," he said, voice low. "I was not designed for attachment. Want is prohibited."

"By the Ledger," Ivy said.

"Yes."

"And what happens if you... want anyway?"

The script beneath his skin flickered.

"Pain," Thorn said. "Correction. Removal."

Her stomach twisted. "Removal?"

"Unbinding," he clarified. "Erasure."

Ivy swallowed hard and finished securing the bandage. She sat back on her heels, suddenly very aware of how close they were—how the space between them felt charged, tight as a drawn wire.

"That's cruel," she said.

"It is efficient."

She scoffed. "You and I have very different definitions of efficient."

Thorn watched her, something strained in his stillness. "You should not concern yourself with my constraints."

"Too late," Ivy said. She stood slowly, then hesitated. "Does it hurt all the time?" she asked.

"No."

"When you're near me?"

His eyes darkened. "Not until now."

Something in her chest clenched.

Without thinking, she reached out. Her palm pressed lightly over the place where the Ledger's script pulsed beneath his skin.

Heat surged. The air crackled, sharp and electric. The Ledger flared, red light blazing through Thorn's chest and throat, script igniting like a living thing awakened.

Thorn gasped, a sound torn from him, and grabbed her wrist but did not pull away.

"Ivy—" His voice broke. "Do not—"

The shop shuddered.

Roses burst open in their buckets, petals unfurling violently. The Ledger Confirmation page appeared on the counter and slammed flat and burned bright.

Ivy's heart thundered. She could feel the connection,

taut and undeniable, like her touch had found a seam in the world and pulled.

She yanked her hand back, breath ragged.

"I'm sorry," she whispered. "I didn't—"

Thorn stared at her, chest heaving, eyes blazing ink-dark in a way she hadn't seen before. The glow beneath his skin dimmed slowly, almost reluctantly.

Silence rushed back in and for a long moment, neither of them moved.

Then Thorn spoke, his voice hoarse with something dangerously close to awe. "You should not be able to do that."

Ivy swallowed, fingers tingling.

His gaze dropped to where her hand had been, then lifted to her face.

"The Ledger recognizes you," he said. "More than before."

Her pulse spiked. "Is that... bad?"

Thorn didn't answer right away. When he did, it was with brutal honesty.

"It is unprecedented."

The word echoed in the quiet shop.

Ivy's breath shook as she exhaled.

"Yeah," she said faintly. "That seems to be a theme." She glanced back at the contract on the counter. "So how many times do I have to touch you to make it stop burning?"

"I do not know," Thorn replied.

Chapter Seven

By midmorning, the shop was a storm. The quiet anticipatory rush of early Valentine shoppers had been obliterated by full-bodied chaos. The bell rang nonstop, voices overlapping, phones buzzing, delivery slips piling up like snowdrifts.

"Name for the card?" Ivy asked, already reaching for ribbon as she balanced the phone against her shoulder.

"—Yes, ma'am, delivery tomorrow between nine and noon—no, we can't guarantee the color of the tulips—"

She scribbled as she spoke, barely looking up. Thorn was already there, sliding a clipboard toward her with the completed order sheet she hadn't realized she'd asked for yet.

"Thank you," she said automatically.

She caught herself a beat later, glancing at him.

He inclined his head. "You are welcome."

The woman at the counter was in her mid-fifties. She was wearing a wool pea-coat, and had kind eyes. She smiled broadly at Thorn.

"Well," she said, approving, "it's about time you hired some help, Ivy."

Ivy froze for half a second.

Thorn did not.

"I am assigned to her," he said calmly.

The woman laughed. "Aren't we all, sweetheart?"

Ivy choked on a breath and turned it into a cough. "Yes. Yes, he's—uh—helping out this week."

"Good," the woman said, leaning closer conspiratorially. "I've worried about you, you know. Working yourself into the ground every February."

Ivy forced a smile. "I'm fine."

The woman waved a dismissive hand. "Sure you are. But it's nice to see someone watching your back."

She glanced at Thorn again, her gaze sliding off him in that strange, instinctive way customers had.

"You picked a quiet one," she added. "Strong, though. And handsome." She winked.

Thorn said nothing.

Ivy rang her up, handed her the receipt, and watched her leave with a bouquet tucked under her arm and a satisfied nod.

The bell jingled again.

Another customer.

Another comment.

"Oh! You finally cloned yourself."

"About time you got an assistant."

"Is he your boyfriend?"

Ivy nearly dropped a bucket.

Thorn's head turned slowly toward her.

Her ears burned. "No."

"I am not," Thorn added, at the same exact moment.

The teenager at the counter snorted. "Awkward."

Ivy shot him a look. "Do you want the roses or not?"

"Yes, ma'am," he said, grinning.

The pace never slowed.

Ivy moved on instinct; she stripped stems, cut, wrap, ring up, answer phone, repeat.

Thorn followed her direction precisely. When she pointed, he moved. When she gestured, he anticipated. When she snapped, "Ribbons." They were already lined up, measured perfectly.

But he handed her buckets, held paper steady, lifted boxes with impossible ease. Customers glanced at his bandaged hand from the Ledger burn and then quickly away.

Something about him set people on edge. Something about him made them feel safe anyway. It was unsettling but it was effective.

By late morning, Ivy was deep in the back cooler grabbing more greenery when Thorn's voice cut through the noise. "Stop."

Ivy's head snapped up.

A teenage boy stood near the display rack, one hand halfway into a bucket of loose roses meant for add-ons. His eyes were wide, caught mid-motion.

"I—I was just—"

"You are stealing," Thorn said.

The boy flinched.

Ivy was already moving. "Just one second..."

"Stealing from a contracted space carries consequence," Thorn continued calmly, stepping forward.

Customers backed away.

The boy swallowed. "I was gonna pay."

"You were not," Thorn said. "The appropriate response is removal."

"Removal?" the boy squeaked.

"Death is acceptable," Thorn added, as if he were recommending a fine.

The shop went completely silent.

Someone gasped.

Ivy reached Thorn in two strides and grabbed his sleeve without thinking. Pain sparked but she ignored it.

"No," she said sharply. "Absolutely not."

Thorn looked down at her hand, then at her face. "He violated—"

"He's a kid," Ivy snapped. "He's scared, broke, and stupid. Not evil."

The boy nodded frantically. "Yes. All of that."

Ivy turned to him. "Put the flowers back."

He immediately opened the cooler door and set the flowers in the bucket.

"Say you're sorry," Ivy demanded.

"I'm sorry," he said, voice cracking.

"And you're leaving," Ivy continued. "If I see you in here again pulling anything like that, you're banned. Understand?"

"Yes, ma'am."

She stepped aside and pointed at the door.

The boy bolted.

The bell jingled violently as he fled.

Silence followed.

A woman near the register cleared her throat. "Well. That escalated."

Ivy plastered on a smile that hurt her face. "Valentine's stress. Poor kid probably had a girlfriend and no money."

A few nervous laughs followed. Business resumed, slower now, like everyone needed to reassure themselves the world was still normal.

Thorn remained very still and it was clear to Ivy that he was battling the concept of *not* killing someone for almost stealing flowers.

When the rush finally thinned and Ivy flipped the sign to "Closed for Lunch", she was so hungry her hands were shaking. She locked the door, leaned her forehead against it for a second, then turned.

Thorn was watching her.

"You undermined enforcement," he said.

She sighed. "I ordered subs. I hope you like Turkey and cheddar cheese with extra pickles."

He blinked. "What?"

"Food," she said, already grabbing her phone. "Humans eat when they're exhausted so they don't pass out."

"I do not—"

"I know," she cut in. "But I do. And you're here and it's rude of me not to offer food. And you had coffee earlier, so you'll have lunch as well."

The delivery arrived quickly—two paper-wrapped subs, a bag of chips, and a soda Ivy immediately cracked open. She perched on the counter and took a long drink.

Thorn stood across from her, posture rigid.

"Why did you let him go?" he asked.

She took a bite, chewed, swallowed. "Because killing someone for stealing flowers is insane."

"He violated ownership," Thorn said. "Ownership is binding."

"Not like that," Ivy replied, staring at the security logo across his chest. "Compassion matters."

"Compassion is inefficient."

"Compassion is human," she said. "So is understanding context. That kid didn't steal because he's bad. He stole because he's desperate."

Thorn considered that, eyes narrowing slightly. "Desperation does not excuse violation."

"No," Ivy agreed. "But death isn't an option. Ever. Not for something like that."

His jaw tightened. "In Hell—"

"I am not in Hell," Ivy said softly. "You're in my shop." She motioned to her surroundings. "This is not hell. This is planet earth. The mortal plane. Whatever you'd call it."

That stopped him. He nodded. "The mortal realm."

She met his gaze, steady despite her exhaustion. "If you're going to help me, you're going to have to learn that humans don't balance every mistake with punishments like death. Sometimes we give warnings. Sometimes we choose mercy."

"And when mercy fails?" Thorn asked.

"Then we try again," Ivy said. "Or we live with the consequences."

He looked at the door, then back at her. "You place value on life disproportionate to harm."

"Yes," she said simply. "That's the point."

Silence stretched.

Finally, Thorn spoke, quieter. "The Ledger would not approve."

Ivy shrugged.

"I am learning," he said slowly, "that your world operates on rules that contradict mine."

Ivy took another bite of her sandwich and smiled tiredly. "Welcome to humanity."

He studied her for a long moment. Then, carefully, he said, "If death is never an option... what is?"

Ivy swallowed, then answered honestly.

"Choice," she said. "And responsibility. And sometimes forgiveness."

Thorn absorbed that in silence.

Outside, the Valentine's banners stirred in the breeze. Inside, a Ledger Demon stood in a flower shop, reconsidering the meaning of consequence.

Chapter Eight

THE EVENING RUSH STARTED QUIETLY WITH ONE phone call, then another, then the bell chiming again and again and again until Ivy stopped noticing it altogether. By five-thirty, every flat surface in the shop was occupied by roses, lilies, tulips and more, in some stage of becoming something meaningful.

"Card for delivery?" Ivy asked, already scribbling.

Thorn slid the clipboard toward her. "Completed. Address confirmed. Payment processed."

She glanced at it and blinked. "When did you—"

"You were speaking," he said. "It seemed efficient to continue."

Her mouth twitched. "You're terrifyingly competent."

"I enforce systems," Thorn replied.

"That explains why you're better at this than most people I've hired and fired."

The bell rang again and the delivery guy, Evan, stepped into the shop. He leaned against the counter like he had all the time in the world, eyes flicking between Ivy and the bundles waiting to be loaded.

"Smells good in here," he said, grinning. "You surviving the rush?"

"Barely," Ivy said honestly, handing him the list. "These go out tonight. Please don't crush the roses. Mr. Jones on Hudson Street lost his mind last week and I had to refund his entire order."

"I'll do my best," Evan said. His gaze lingered on her face a second too long. "You look tired again. You should let someone take you out after this week. You know... relax a little."

Thorn went still as stone.

Ivy was already reaching for the receipt printer and calculating tomorrow's order count.

"That's kind of you," she said, polite and distant. "But I don't really have time for going out."

"She's unavailable." The voice was calm and precise.

The temperature in the shop dipped.

Evan blinked and looked at Thorn, laughter faltering. "Uh. Sorry, man. I didn't realize—"

"Ivy is unavailable," Thorn repeated, stepping closer.

Ivy turned sharply. "Thorn."

His gaze didn't leave Evan. "Your attention is unwelcome."

Evan raised both hands. "Okay. Cool. Just trying to be friendly." He glanced at Thorn then to Ivy. "You sure you need security here?"

"Friendliness is not required to deliver flowers," Thorn said.

"Okay, that's enough," Ivy said firmly, stepping between them. "Delivery list. Boxes. Go."

Evan grabbed the stack faster than necessary, eyes darting. "Right. Yeah. See you tomorrow. Take care, Ivy."

He all but fled and the bell jingled violently behind him.

Ivy exhaled slowly and turned to Thorn. "What was that?"

He looked at her then, something tight beneath his stillness. "He was attempting to claim your attention."

"So?"

"So that is... problematic."

She stared. "You don't get to police who talks to me."

"I am not policing," Thorn said. "I am responding."

"To what?" Ivy pressed.

He hesitated as dark eyes roamed over her. That alone set her nerves humming.

"The binding," he said at last. "It establishes priority."

Her chest tightened. "Priority does not mean ownership."

"No," Thorn said. "But it does produce... resistance."

"Resistance," she repeated with a soft laugh. "That's a funny word for jealousy."

"I do not experience jealousy," Thorn said immediately.

"Sure about that?" She folded her arms. "You just scared off a delivery driver because he flirted with me. Evan always flirts. The customers like it. And you've been here for five minutes. You don't get to chase people away from me. I've known Evan for years."

"He was inefficient. You needed him to deliver the flowers competently."

"That is not what I meant." She stopped and rubbed her forehead. "Okay. Are you feeling... weird? Is this from the contract?"

His brow creased faintly. "Define weird."

"Like you don't like it when people get close to me? Possessive?" She wanted to touch his forehead and see if he had a fever, his cheeks were flushed but it was warm in the shop.

His silence was answer enough.

"The Ledger amplifies attachment," he said carefully. "I will control it."

Ivy searched his face, looking for heat, for hunger, for something she could name. What she found instead was restraint stretched thin.

"Okay," she said quietly. "Just... don't do that again. I can handle myself. And I need Evan. Don't scare him off."

He inclined his head, dark hair falling over his eyes. "Understood." He looked away. "You have customers."

Customers poured in a rush of last-minute orders, desperate faces, and whispered confessions scribbled onto cards. Ivy moved like a current through it all, Thorn at her side, anticipating without being asked. He lifted boxes, recorded orders, fetched supplies. When Ivy reached automatically for something, it was already there. Somehow he knew and for a split second she wondered if it had something to do with the contract. It must.

By the time she locked the door for the final time that night, her body felt hollowed out and buzzing at once.

"That was insane." She leaned against the counter and laughed softly. "I don't think I could've gotten through today without you."

Thorn watched her, gaze steady. "Your gratitude is noted."

"I mean it," she said. "You helped. A lot. A lot more than anyone ever has in my life."

"You did not collapse from exhaustion," he said. "That was the objective."

She smiled tiredly. "You have a very low bar for success."

They cleaned in companionable quiet, the shop settling around them. When Ivy finally turned off the lights and grabbed her keys, she paused, looking at him.

Thorn had taken off the security vest and rolled up his sleeves.

Ivy bit her lip and closed her eyes, taking a deep breath before she offered something outrageous.

"You can't just stand there all night," she said, motioning to the window.

"I can," Thorn replied.

"I know you can," she said. "But you don't have to."

She hesitated, then gestured toward the stairs. "I have a couch. It's not great, but you can rest on it."

Thorn's eyes lifted to the ceiling, as if he could see through it. "You are offering me rest."

"Sort of," Ivy said. "I know you don't sleep."

"I do not."

"But you look tired."

He considered that. "I am."

Her brows knit. "You just said—"

"I do not sleep," Thorn said. "But I am not accustomed to prolonged presence in the mortal realm."

"How long have you been here?" she asked.

"Days," he said. "Which is... unprecedented."

"And why are you tired?"

"The binding," Thorn said. "The Ledger is active, like a living creature. It requires constant recalibration. It is always thinking."

Ivy swallowed. "So it's... draining you."

"Yes."

She unlocked the apartment door and stepped aside. "Then you're sleeping on the couch. Or... not sleeping. Resting. Whatever you call it. You can just lay there in the darkness with your eyes open."

Thorn hesitated only a moment before nodding and saying, "Okay."

He followed her upstairs. Ivy wondered why his presence no longer frightened her. He was much bigger than she was, and she had run up the stairs with fear tingling up her back with nothing behind her before. Now the climb seemed relaxed, protected. As she unlocked the door handle, she steeped in the warmth of his body being so close to her. Maybe it had to do with the contract and how he was bound to the flower shop?

She opened the door. "Home sweet home."

The apartment was quiet, warm, and lived-in. Ivy kicked off her shoes and dropped her bag, suddenly aware of how small the space was and how close he felt in it.

She grabbed a hair tie out of a bowl near the door and twisted her hair up in a bun. She walked to the kitchen and opened the fridge. There weren't many options but her gaze settled on steak that should have been cooked yesterday and lettuce she'd need to cut the brown spots off of.

"I'm guessing if you ate steak, you'd like it rare?" Ivy

took the packages out of the fridge and reached into the cupboards for a cutting board and pan.

Thorn stood near the edge of the living space. His security vest was folded neatly over the back of a chair and the top button of his shirt was undone. The shadows that clung to him had loosened, thinning in the lamplight, but they hadn't vanished entirely.

"You don't have to just... stand there," Ivy said, glancing at him and trying not to stare. "You can sit."

"I am capable of standing."

She snorted. "I'm capable of surviving on caffeine and spite, but that doesn't mean it's ideal."

She set the cutting board down near the sink and dug a knife out of the drawer.

Thorn said nothing but he moved, settling onto the edge of the couch as if he were testing the concept of furniture.

Ivy smiled to herself and turned back to the stove. She poured olive oil into the pan and turned the heat on.

"I'm making steak salad," she said. "Because it's fast and I don't have the energy for dishes."

He watched her hands. "You prepare nourishment despite exhaustion."

"Yeah," she said. "It's called being alive."

She flipped the steak and reached for the greens. After a moment, she added casually, "You can shower if you want. There are towels in the hall closet."

Thorn's gaze snapped up. "Shower."

"Yes. Water. Soap. Shampoo. Please don't tell me you never shower." She hesitated. "I don't have clean clothes for you, though."

"That will not be an issue," he said. "And I shower."

Ivy frowned. "You don't own clothes."

"They will arrive."

She opened her mouth, then closed it again. "I'm not even going to ask."

"That is wise."

She gestured vaguely toward the bathroom. "Go ahead. I'll be done in a few."

Thorn stood, pausing as if orienting himself, then disappeared down the short hall.

A moment later, Ivy heard the shower turn on. She froze, knife halfway through a cucumber. The sound was startlingly intimate.

She shook her head, cheeks warm, and focused on the meal as she washed greens, whisked dressing, and plated it all with care. It had been so long since she'd had a dinner guest. As she worked, her thoughts kept drifting in directions she didn't entirely trust. She liked him being here, as strange as it was.

This wasn't supposed to feel like this. This was a demon. A Ledger Demon. Something she had no clue ever existed. She'd seen his fangs though, and he definitely wasn't human.

But he helped her work. He noticed when she was tired. He seemed to care.

The apartment felt different with him in it; less hollow, less like she was always bracing for something to fall apart and having to deal with it completely alone.

She swallowed hard and set the table for two. She reached for a bottle of wine and grabbed two glasses. She hesitated, then shrugged. "Why not?" she murmured before pouring.

The shower shut off.

A few minutes later, Thorn emerged.

Ivy turned just in time to see him step into the living area wearing something that looked like black linen loungewear, hair damp, sleeves rolled up, collar open. The script beneath his skin had dimmed, the lines less angry. He looked refreshed. Dangerous in a quieter way.

She forgot how to breathe for a second.

"You look," she cleared her throat, "less like you're about to audit my soul."

"The water was effective," Thorn said.

"Good," she said, gesturing toward the table. "Dinner's ready."

They sat.

Ivy took a bite and nearly groaned. "Oh thank God," she said. "I was worried I'd ruined it. I don't usually eat it this rare but it's good."

Thorn followed her lead, tasting carefully. His eyes flickered with surprise. "This is... excellent."

She smiled, warmth spreading through her chest. "High praise from Hell. What do you typically eat for dinner? Oh, wait." She flushed, remembering the fangs.

"Blood."

"Like a vampire?"

He was watching her intensely. "Do you know much about vampirism?"

She shook her head. "Only the fictional ones." Her eyes narrowed. "Vampires are fiction in my world, as well as contracts that steal your soul."

"Blood rituals are as old as time. Angels, demons, gods have all consumed blood to survive. Some have strayed from the practice, but in Hell it's how we survive. For some, the blood bonds them for life and they cannot live without each other."

"So you kill people and drain their blood?" Ivy swallowed hard.

"No. It only takes a small amount. I have never killed for blood consumption." He tapped his fork. "But stealing. Yes. I have killed for that."

Shock tore through Ivy and she coughed mid-swallow, choking on her food.

"I've scared you. I apologize." Thorn reached out and smacked her on the back once and it cleared her throat. "Maybe don't ask me about the blood. I am compelled to answer you."

Ivy nodded as she took a drink of the wine.

They ate in companionable quiet, broken only by the clink of forks. Thorn watched her more than his plate, as if cataloging her every movement. When they finished, Ivy stood and reached for the dishes.

"No," Thorn said.

She paused. "No?"

"You will rest," he said, already collecting plates. "I will clean."

She laughed. "Do you even know how?"

He considered the sink. "It is not complex."

"That's what everyone says before they flood the kitchen."

His gaze slid to her, dry. "I manage infernal systems."

"Okay," she conceded. "Fair." She raised her hands in

surrender. She stood but lingered a moment, watching him rinse a plate with meticulous care, then softened.

"Thank you," she said quietly.

He glanced at her. "For what?"

"For today. For... all of it."

Something unreadable passed through his expression.

"You should go prepare for sleep," he said gently. "You are beyond your limits."

She nodded, suddenly very tired again. "I will."

As she turned toward the bathroom, she added lightly, "Don't reorganize my cabinets."

"I will respect existing systems."

She smiled, disappearing down the hall.

Ivy stood beneath the shower spray, head tipped back, letting the heat beat against her shoulders and neck, trying to rinse the day off her skin. The shop's noise still rang in her ears—bells, voices, Thorn's calm directives cutting through it all like a blade.

And then there was the moment Evan tried to ask her to dinner and Thorn stepped in.

Ivy is unavailable.

The water ran hotter. She braced her hands against the tile and exhaled slowly.

That hadn't been enforcement. Not really. That had been... something else; possession in a way that made her stomach flip and her brain short-circuit.

Jealousy.

Except Thorn had said he didn't experience jealousy.

Which meant either he was wrong... or the binding was doing something far more dangerous than she wanted to admit.

She closed her eyes.

The binding establishes priority.

Her pulse kicked.

And then there was the other thing.

Blood.

He'd said it so casually earlier, when she'd asked what Ledger Demons survived on. Not food, not water. Blood-drawn from contracts, from breaches, from the moment something living realized it had lost.

Like a vampire.

She snorted softly to herself under the spray, half hysterical.

Great, you invited a vampire in.

Except it was worse than that. She had unknowingly invited in a Ledger Demon. He was something ancient and lethal and bound by laws she barely understood and she had offered him her couch.

The water coursed down her arms, over the faint scars from the sharp edges of the flower stems she barely noticed anymore. Her life had always been about quiet, relentless survival. Keep the shop afloat. Keep the lights on. Don't ask for help because help came with strings. And no regrets.

And yet—

He'd helped.

He'd stood at her side all day, silent and watchful. He'd taken direction without complaint. He'd noticed her shaking before she had. He'd ordered her lunch like it was non-negotiable.

He'd looked at her like she mattered.

Ivy shut off the water and stepped out, wrapping herself in a towel before the chill could creep in. The shower steamed the bathroom until the mirror vanished. She dressed quickly in old soft pajamas pants and a threadbare T-shirt that was nearly see through. She paused in front of the mirror. Her reflection looked the same. Her life had changed very drastically in just a few days.

"This is insane," she murmured to herself.

She left the bathroom and padded down the short hallway, heart thudding just a little harder than necessary. The apartment was quiet, lights low. The faint sound of movement came from the kitchen.

Thorn stood at the sink, washing the last plate from dinner with methodical care. The counters were clean. The pan from cooking steak was dried and set on the stove.

She leaned against the doorway, watching him.

A demon. A blood-drinker. A creature who got jealous over a florist and a delivery guy. He was bound to the shop.

And she felt... safe. Last time she had let a guy into her life like this, it had been ruinous.

"You're thinking too hard," Thorn said without turning.

She startled. "It's rude to assume," she teased.

"I observe patterns," he replied. "I did not assume."

She crossed her arms, suddenly very aware of how thin the line was between fear and fascination.

"You said earlier," she began slowly, "that your kind survives on blood."

He studied her for a long moment. "Are you afraid?"

She searched herself honestly.

The answer unsettled her.

"No," she said quietly. "I probably should be. But I'm not."

The script beneath his skin pulsed faintly, like something listening.

"That may change," Thorn said.

"Maybe," Ivy agreed. "But right now it's just strange."

She gestured vaguely between them. "You being here. Watching out for me. Getting jealous."

"I said I would control that," he replied.

She smiled faintly. "I know." She hesitated, then added, "You didn't scare me, by the way. With the delivery guy."

His brow creased. "I did not intend to."

"I know." She yawned, fatigue finally catching up. "I just wanted you to know."

Silence settled between them.

"Well," Ivy said at last, pushing off the doorframe, "I'm going to bed. Try not to drink anyone while I'm asleep."

"I will not," Thorn said immediately.

She paused, smirked. "That was a joke."

"I was aware."

"Liar."

"I did not lie."

She laughed softly and turned toward the living room. She grabbed a blanket from the back of the couch and when she turned he was directly behind her.

"In case you get cold."

She handed him the blanket. Their fingers brushed.

Heat flared, gentle this time and neither of them screamed in pain.

"Goodnight, Thorn," she said softly.

He looked at the couch, then at her. "Thank you."

"For what?"

"For recognizing fatigue," he said. "It is not a courtesy I am often granted."

Her chest ached at that, sharp and unwanted.

"Yeah," she murmured. "Well. Get used to it."

She turned toward her bedroom, then paused.

"And Thorn?"

"Yes."

"Try not to threaten to kill anyone."

He considered. "I will attempt neutrality." His head tipped to the side. "Wait."

Ivy went still.

"Come here."

Her feet moved before she could think.

"Show me your hand."

Ivy held up her right hand.

"The other one," he clarified.

She held up her left hand.

His fingers wrapped around her wrist and turned her palm so that he could see the pad of her thumb.

"How long have you suffered with this injury?"

Confusion struck and then Ivy remembered the thorn that had gotten stuck in her thumb the other day. "I've been trying to get it out but it's too deep."

"Would you like me to remove it?" he asked.

"I didn't know you were a doctor."

"Not a doctor."

"Oh, well. Sure. It's been bothering me."

Thorn pulled her hand closer and folded her fingers down. His mouth wrapped around her thumb and she felt teeth and a gentle pull.

Her eyes widened and she went still at the feel of his lips against her skin. She opened her mouth but no sound came out.

He was watching her the entire time. And just as quickly as it started, he released her hand and pulled the thorn from between his front teeth.

"Uh, thanks," Ivy finally said as Thorn walked to the kitchen and rinsed the sliver down the drain.

"Goodnight, Ivy." He didn't turn around when he said it.

Ivy backed away and nearly ran to her bedroom. She closed the door then leaned against it, breathing heavy. What the heck was that? And why did her body feel like it was on fire?

It was night and a Ledger Demon lay on a mortal couch, staring at the ceiling, feeling something dangerously close to peace and blaming the binding for every second of it.

Chapter Nine

When Ivy's alarm went off it was still dark outside. The sound cut through her sleep like a blade, sharp and unforgiving, lifting her from a very strange dream about Dracula.

She groaned, slapped at her phone, and lay there for a second, staring at the ceiling.

Valentine's Day was in three days.

She had to move. Her body protested as she swung her legs over the side of the bed. Everything ached. She brushed her teeth and washed her face, then dug through her closet and pulled on jeans and a sweater. She twisted her hair into a messy knot and rubbed at the faint lines under her eyes in the mirror.

As she stepped into the hallway, something stopped her cold. She smelled coffee. She padded into the kitchen, heart suddenly loud in her chest.

Thorn stood at the counter. The overhead light was on, the apartment still wrapped in gray shadow. He was dressed in the security clothes again. A mug sat on the counter with steam curling from it.

A pan sizzled softly on the stove. She smelled eggs, toast, and something green like spinach.

Ivy stopped in the doorway.

"You're... awake," she said stupidly.

Thorn turned. "You were scheduled to rise at five forty."

She blinked. "You checked my alarm?"

"I heard it," he said. "And then analyzed your routine."

"That's..." She stopped herself, exhaling. "Okay. Fair."

She stepped closer, eyes on the mug. "Is that my coffee?"

"Yes."

She picked it up automatically, took a cautious sip and closed her eyes. Honey. Milk. Exactly the right balance and temperature.

"I didn't tell you how I make it," she said softly.

"You made me some yesterday," Thorn replied. "It was easy to tell what you'd added to it."

Her throat tightened. She swallowed, then took another sip. "This is unsettling."

He inclined his head. "Noted. Next time I will surprise you with something different."

Her gaze dropped to the pan. "You also cooked."

"Yes."

"I don't usually eat this early," she said reflexively, setting the mug down. "I'll grab something later."

"No," Thorn said. The word landed with gentle authority.

She looked up at him, brows knitting. "No?"

"You were depleted last night," he said. "Your reaction time slowed. Your hands trembled. You ignored pain. That sliver in your thumb was close to infection."

She opened her mouth to argue and stopped. Because he wasn't wrong.

"You will eat," Thorn continued, sliding a plate toward her. "Exhaustion compromises your ability to function. It will be a busy day."

Ivy stared at the plate. Then at him.

"You can't just order me around," she said, but there was no real heat in it.

"I am not ordering," Thorn replied. "I am preventing recurrence."

She huffed a laugh. "That sounds like an order."

His gaze softened, just a fraction. "It is concern."

That did it. Ivy sighed, shoulders slumping. "You're very annoying."

"I have been told this."

She sat, fork in hand, and took a tentative bite of the food he'd cooked. It was good.

"Okay," she admitted. "This is good."

Thorn watched her eat with quiet focus, as if this were as important as any contract he'd ever enforced.

She glanced up at him. "You don't have to hover."

"I am ensuring compliance," he said calmly.

She smirked. "You're enjoying this."

A pause. Then, carefully, "Perhaps. I have never watched mortals eat breakfast like this before."

She smiled into her coffee.

Outside, the sky lightened, dawn creeping in slow and inevitable. Another long day waited for her with orders, customers, and—she was sure—chaos. But for the first time in a long while, Ivy wasn't starting it alone.

"Thorn," Ivy said as she looked up at him.

"Yes?"

"Don't surprise me with the coffee made differently. That's a day ender."

Thorn nodded as he said, "Noted."

THE STAIRWELL WAS COLD. NOT THE MILD, EARLY-morning chill Ivy expected, but a sharp, bone-deep cold that crawled under her sweater and settled there. She pulled her arms tighter around herself as she and Thorn descended, keys already in her hand.

"Did you turn the heat off?" she muttered.

"No," Thorn said.

Ivy slowed as she made it to the bottom of the stairs, the cold sharpening, the air heavy and wrong. Her steps faltered on the last stair.

"I don't like this," she whispered.

Thorn moved in front of her instinctively, one hand lifting as if to shield her. "Stay behind me."

She opened her mouth to argue but then she saw the front window was shattered.

Glass glittered across the wooden floors like ice, the display completely destroyed. The door hung crooked in its frame, wood splintered, lock torn free. Ivy stepped closer and noticed overturned buckets lay on their sides, water soaking into the floor. Flowers—*her flowers*—were ripped apart, stems snapped, petals shredded and scattered like confetti from a celebration gone cruel.

Ivy stopped breathing. "No," she whispered.

Her keys slipped from her fingers and hit the floor with a sharp, useless sound. She took one step forward, then another, and then the weight of it all hit her at once.

Her knees buckled but Thorn caught her before she fell, steady hands bracing her as her body shook violently. He helped her to the chair.

"I can't," she choked, tears blinding her. "I can't survive this. I won't make it through the year. I can't pay the suppliers, I can't fulfill the orders. Valentine's Day is ruined." Her voice broke completely as the reality crushed down on her chest. "This is it," she sobbed. "This is where it ends. I will never financially recover from this."

Thorn's anger was immediate and terrifying.

The shadows surged, curling tight around his frame. The script beneath his skin flared, red-hot and furious, the Ledger reacting to the violation of its claim. The temperature dropped another degree, frost ghosting across the broken glass.

"They trespassed," Thorn said, voice low and lethal. "They damaged collateral."

"I don't care about the collateral," Ivy cried. "I care about my life. My shop. Everything I've built. It's all gone. I can't fix this."

He turned her gently to face him.

"It will be okay," he said.

She shook her head, tears streaking down her cheeks.

"Don't say that. You don't understand. One bad week, one setback, and I'm done."

"I understand," Thorn said.

She laughed brokenly. "You don't."

"I do," he replied, unwavering. "Because I am bound to protect this place." His hands tightened just slightly on her arms. "This shop will not fall," Thorn said. "Not while the binding stands."

Ivy wiped her face with the heel of her hand, breath hitching. She bent, picked up the broom from beside the counter.

"Then we clean," she said. "And I call the police."

Thorn was already moving.

While Ivy dialed the phone with shaking fingers, Thorn swept through the shop with frightening efficiency. He gathered unbroken flowers, trimming their damaged edges with precision. He lifted shattered cooler doors, stretching heavy plastic sheeting from storage across the openings to trap the cold inside.

The Ledger glowed faintly as he worked.

Ivy heard him speaking quietly into her shop phone while she cleaned up glass.

"Yes," Thorn said. "Immediate replacement. Priority delivery. Within hours."

She stared at him. "Who are you calling?"

"Your suppliers," he replied. "And their suppliers."

Her breath caught. "I don't think they can help."

"They will," Thorn said.

And somehow, impossibly, they did.

Within minutes, confirmation texts lit up Ivy's phone. Emergency deliveries. Partial credit. Deferred payment.

We've got you.
We heard about the vandalization.
Hang in there.
We look out for our own.

The police arrived. A report was filed. Photos were taken.

It all happened so fast that Ivy barely had a moment to process any of it.

Then something unexpected happened.

People came.

Mrs. Hensley from two blocks over, breathless and worried. "Are you okay, dear?" she asked. "I saw the broken windows when I unlocked my shop." She was gripping Ivy's hand. "Did you get hurt?"

"No. No, Mrs. Hensley, I'm fine. It happened during the night."

Mrs. Hensley nodded then glanced at Thorn. "I heard you'd hired security. Best schedule a night shift one too. This world isn't what it used to be."

Mrs. Hensley picked up a petite vase with lilies and baby's breath. "This will look nice at my place."

Ivy rang her out, thankful that the power and cash register were still working. Whoever busted up the shop wasn't after money.

"Take care, sweetheart," Mrs. Hensley said as she left.

The café owner, Dan, from around the corner stopped by next with a tray of muffins and a thermos of coffee.

"We heard," Dan said, looking around the shop. "Sure glad you weren't hurt."

Then a regular who'd bought flowers every Valentine's Day for his late wife stood silently in the doorway, eyes soft.

"Are you okay?" he asked.

Ivy nodded, voice raw but steady. "We're fixing it."

Thorn stood behind her, silent and immovable, a dark presence that made people uneasy but he also made them linger, reassured by the fact that she wasn't alone.

By midmorning, the shop was in full swing again, the mess cleaned up and the broken windows sealed with plastic and tape. Orders were rewritten. The bell rang as customers came in to buy, to check on her, to help, and to remind her she mattered.

Ivy looked around at the mess, the work, the people, the impossible man at her side and felt something solid settle in her chest. She hadn't been broken. She had been defended.

CHAPTER TEN

THE FLOWER DELIVERY TRUCK ARRIVED JUST after noon.

Ivy heard the low grind of an engine slowing out front and the hiss of air brakes. For one wild second she was certain it would be another disappointment, another almost, another *we tried*. Then the back doors opened and buckets upon buckets of flowers filled the sidewalk. Roses wrapped in brown paper. Crates of greenery. Boxes marked with bold Sharpie notes: *RUSH. PRIORITY. HANDLE WITH CARE.*

Ivy looked at Thorn.

"Oh my god," she breathed.

But Thorn was already moving. He crossed the shop in long strides, lifting crates as if they weighed nothing, and carried them inside with ruthless efficiency.

"These go into the cooler first," Ivy said, snapping back into motion. "Roses on the left, greenery on the right. Watch the eucalyptus, it bruises easily."

"I will be careful," Thorn said.

They worked like they'd done this for years. Ivy trimmed stems and assessed for damage while Thorn hauled, sorted, and refilled buckets with surgical precision. He memorized the cooler layout in minutes. When she said, "hand me the shears," they were already in his palm.

Orders resumed as if the break-in had never happened.

One of Ivy's regulars was at the counter; a gray-haired and sharp-eyed woman who watched Thorn move between stations.

"He's a good one," she said quietly to Ivy. "You keeping him?"

Ivy flushed. "He's just helping."

The woman smiled knowingly. "That's how it starts."

Thorn met the woman at the door as she was leaving. "You are familiar with this area."

"I've lived here forty years," she said proudly.

"I require nourishment for Ivy," Thorn said. "What is suitable for midday?"

The woman blinked, then brightened. "Salads from Luca's Deli. The big ones. They're loaded with protein. You'll want extra dressing. She likes ranch."

Thorn nodded once. "Thank you."

He went to the phone before Ivy could stop him, placed the order with brisk clarity, and hung up.

She stared at him. "You just... ordered lunch."

"Yes."

"Without asking me."

"You forget to eat," Thorn said. "I will not allow it today."

She opened her mouth to argue and closed it again, too tired to pretend she didn't appreciate it.

"Thank you."

Thorn nodded before getting back to work.

The bell rang again. And again.

Ivy's back ached. Her feet screamed. She didn't slow down until Thorn gently but firmly took a bouquet from her hands that she was trying to finish.

"You will sit," he said.

"I'm fine."

"You are shaking."

She looked down. She was.

"I can finish this one," she protested weakly.

"You have finished many," Thorn said. "Now you will eat."

He guided her, strong hand pressed against the small of her back, leading her toward the stool by the counter and set a salad in front of her when the deli delivery arrived moments later.

She stared at it. "Did you time that?"

"Yes."

She huffed a laugh and took a bite.

Thorn took over seamlessly.

Customers barely noticed the shift. If anything, the shop seemed calmer with him running the front. His presence was authoritative enough to keep lines orderly, his voice steady as he confirmed orders and delivery windows.

Ivy watched him between bites, something warm and disorienting blooming in her chest.

She had never trusted anyone enough to take over like this before.

The sound of tools clanking outside pulled her attention to the front window. Two men in work jackets unloaded equipment. One of them glanced in, waved, and held up a clipboard.

"Glass replacement," he called through the open door. "Emergency order."

Ivy nearly dropped her fork.

"What?" She scrambled off the stool and rushed forward. "Already?"

"Yeah," the man said. "Your insurance paid to rush it. We'll have it done in an hour."

She turned slowly to Thorn. Her voice trembled. "How?"

"The Ledger recognizes disruption to protected assets," Thorn replied. "Correction was... prioritized."

Her eyes burned. This was too much. Too fast. Too generous. She pressed her lips together and nodded, because if she spoke she might cry again.

The glass went in quickly. The men worked efficiently and they were respectful and quiet as customers entered the store around them. By the time Ivy finished her salad, the shop was whole again with the front windows gleaming, the door frame reinforced, and locks reset.

Sunlight poured in like it had never been interrupted.

Ivy leaned against the counter and let out a breath she felt like she'd been holding for years.

"I can't believe this," she whispered.

Thorn stood beside her, gaze sweeping the restored shop. "You should. You signed the contract, after all."

The bell rang again.

Another customer.

Another order.

Ivy straightened, squared her shoulders, and reached for ribbon.

"Okay," she said, voice steadier now. "Let's finish this."

Thorn inclined his head.

And together, they set to work.

Ivy sat on the stool behind the counter, calculator in hand, receipts spread like fallen leaves. The shop was dim except for the register lamp and the soft glow of the cooler. Outside, the sky had gone deep blue, the last of the foot traffic thinning to nothing and it had started snowing.

Her shoulders ached. Her eyes burned. But the numbers... the numbers were good. Not miraculous. Not life-changing. But *good*. Enough orders filled. Enough deliveries scheduled. Enough cash flow to keep breathing.

She exhaled slowly and set the calculator down.

"We survived the day," she murmured.

Across the shop, Thorn was checking the locks, and he tested the reinforced door. Every motion was like he was sealing something sacred.

"Today concludes favorably," he said.

Ivy smiled faintly. "That might be the nicest thing anyone's ever said to me about a Tuesday."

The bell over the door chimed and Ivy stiffened.

Thorn turned instantly but relaxed a bit when two uniformed officers stepped inside.

"Evening," one of the officers said. "You Ivy Calder?"

"Yes," Ivy replied, heart kicking up again. "Is everything okay?"

"We wanted to update you on the vandalism report from the earlier today," the officer said. "We caught the person responsible."

Ivy's breath caught. "You did?"

"Yes, ma'am. Turns out the restaurant across the street has exterior cameras. Clear view of the window and door."

The second officer held up a phone.

"We think you might recognize him."

The screen turned toward her.

Ivy's stomach dropped.

It was the same teenage boy from two days ago; the one Thorn had stopped mid-theft, the one Ivy had sent away with a warning instead of something worse. She stared at the image, her chest tightening.

She whispered, "He tried to steal flowers earlier this week."

The officers exchanged a look.

"He admitted to it," one said. "Said he was angry. Didn't think anyone would get hurt."

Ivy swallowed. "Is he okay?"

"Shaken," the officer said. "But unharmed. His parents have been notified. Charges are being discussed but given his age and lack of record... we'll see what happens."

A low voice cut through the air.

"He should have been killed."

The temperature in the shop dropped sharply.

The officers stiffened.

Ivy turned slowly.

Thorn stood near the door, shadows coiled tight around his feet.

"He violated a protected space," Thorn said, voice calm and deadly. "He inflicted damage after being warned. The appropriate consequence was termination."

The officers stared.

Ivy's heart slammed into her ribs.

"Thorn," she said sharply. "Don't mind him he's from a place with much more strict laws."

"I am stating fact," he said. "Mercy created escalation."

Her eyes widened. "He's a kid."

"He is a liability," Thorn replied.

The officers shifted uneasily.

"Uh," one of them said carefully, "we'll... continue processing this through the proper channels."

"Yes," Ivy said quickly. "Thank you for letting me know. Don't mind my friend here, he's a little... extra."

They nodded, gave Thorn one last uncertain glance, and left.

The bell jingled softly behind them.

Silence flooded back in.

Ivy pressed her palms to the counter and breathed until her hands stopped shaking.

"You cannot say things like that," she said quietly.

Thorn's jaw tightened. "It is accurate."

"It's not acceptable," she shot back. "Not here. Not ever."

"He destroyed what you built," Thorn said. "He threatened your survival."

"And killing him wouldn't fix that," Ivy snapped. "It wouldn't fix anything."

He looked at her, something conflicted flickering beneath his skin. "You warned him. He returned with violence."

"Yes," Ivy said, voice cracking. "And now he'll face consequences. Real ones. That's how this works."

Thorn was silent.

She softened her tone, exhaustion bleeding through. "You don't get to decide who deserves to die."

His gaze lowered slightly, as if that truth pressed somewhere unfamiliar.

"The Ledger disagrees," he said.

"I don't care," Ivy replied. "I didn't bind myself to the Ledger."

The words hung between them.

Finally, Thorn spoke. "Then your world is... inefficient."

Ivy laughed weakly. "Yeah. It is."

She gathered the receipts, squared the stack, and stood. "But it's where I live. I didn't get to choose."

Thorn nodded once.

"I am applying Hell's law to a mortal structure," he said aloud, testing the truth of it on his tongue. "That is the error. I will adjust," he said. "I will not apply terminal consequence where it is not required," Thorn said. "I will not enforce Hell's finality upon those who are still learning how to exist."

The script under his skin flared.

"I will control it," Thorn said, echoing the promise he had made before.

"Good." Ivy nodded. "Thank you."

Chapter Eleven

Ivy stood beneath the shower spray longer than she meant to, forehead against the tile, eyes closed as the heat worked its way into her muscles. The shop. The police. The numbers. Thorn's voice threaded through it all. He was steady, terrifying, and protective.

She was so tired.

When she finally shut off the water and dressed, her hair was still damp and loose down her back. She rubbed her eyes and stepped into the hallway, already bracing for the quiet. Instead, she smelled food.

Her steps slowed.

The kitchen light was on. Thorn stood at the stove, sleeves rolled, posture relaxed in a way she still wasn't used to seeing. A pan sizzled softly. The table was set with two plates, two glasses, a bottle of wine uncorked and breathing like he'd looked up how long it should sit.

Ivy stopped in the doorway.

"You're cooking again," she said.

"Yes."

"Is that salmon?"

"It is."

She laughed quietly, disbelief and exhaustion tangling together. "You just keep doing things I don't expect."

"I am adapting," Thorn replied.

She crossed the room and leaned against the counter, watching him move. He worked carefully, tasting nothing, adjusting by scent and instinct alone. When he plated the salmon, rice, and roasted carrots, it looked ridiculously appetizing.

"I didn't know you were a chef," Ivy said with a smile.

Thorn paused, looking at her. "Does my cooking make you happy?"

Ivy smiled wider. "Good food usually makes me happy."

"Perfect." He motioned to her chair.

They ate together in the low light, the apartment wrapped in evening hush.

Ivy took a bite and sighed. "This is really good. This stuff isn't from my fridge. Did you go shopping while I was in the shower?"

"I had groceries delivered. You were almost out of coffee so I ordered more of that as well."

"You learn really quickly."

Thorn watched her with focused attention, like her reaction mattered more than the outcome. "I am pleased to make you happy."

He poured wine.

"Thank you," she said softly.

"For the wine?"

"For all of it," she said, gesturing vaguely. "I've never had someone like you in my life."

He inclined his head. "You are... observable."

She smiled at that and took a sip, warmth spreading through her chest.

"I wish," she said suddenly, without quite meaning to, "that you were real to my world. I'd keep you around."

The words hung between them.

Thorn frowned. "I am real."

She blinked. "You know what I mean."

"I do not," he said.

She studied his face in the quiet, the candlelight catching the planes of him, the faint script beneath his skin. He looked... off. Paler than before, drawn like her comment had sucked the life out of him.

"Thorn," she said carefully. "Are you okay?"

"Yes."

She narrowed her eyes. "That answer was too fast."

He hesitated before saying, "I believe," he said slowly, "that the mortal realm is altering my state."

Her stomach tightened. "Altering how?"

"I have never remained this long," he said. "Nor been bound to the Ledger in this manner. The feedback is... inconsistent."

She watched him closely—mainly the way his tongue ran briefly across his teeth. The thought landed cold and sharp. Hunger.

"You've been here for days," Ivy said quietly. "You said your kind feeds on blood."

His gaze snapped to hers. "Do not ask me that."

Her heart started to pound. "Thorn—"

"No," he said, firmer now. "Do not."

She stood slowly, moving closer before she could talk herself out of it. Her pulse was loud in her ears, but her voice came out steady.

"You're changing," she said. "And I don't know how to help you."

"I do not require assistance."

"That's not true," Ivy said. "You help me constantly. It's only fair that I help you." She lifted her wrist. "You can bite me," she said. "As long as you don't drain me."

The air went electric.

Thorn rose instantly, chair scraping softly as he backed away like she'd drawn a blade. The shadows surged, coiling tight around him; the script beneath his skin flared hot and angry.

"No," he said, voice rough. "You do not understand what you are asking."

Her arm trembled, but she didn't lower it. "I think I understand enough."

"You do not," Thorn repeated. He turned his face away from her wrist, jaw clenched hard, the muscles moving. "I cannot hurt you. I cannot take from you. Not you. Not this place."

"I'm offering," she said.

"That is what makes it dangerous," he snapped.

He looked back at her then, eyes dark and strained, hunger and restraint locked in violent opposition.

"It would be safer," Thorn said tightly, "for me to go without blood than to risk what that would do—to you, to me, to the binding."

Ivy lowered her arm slowly, heart aching in a way she hadn't expected.

"Okay," she whispered. "Okay. I won't push."

Thorn turned away, bracing his hands on the counter, shoulders rigid. "Do not offer yourself like that again."

She nodded. "I'm sorry."

Silence stretched between them but it was heavy and charged, intimate in a way that made her breath shallow.

When he finally spoke again, his voice was quieter. "I do not know what I am becoming," Thorn said. "And that is… unsettling."

Ivy stepped closer. "Yeah," she said softly. "You seem a little different than the first night you visited here."

He huffed a sound that might have been a laugh, if Ledger Demons laughed.

They finished dinner in careful quiet.

Later, as Ivy rinsed her glass and headed for bed, she glanced back once more.

Thorn stood alone in the kitchen, pale and watchful, shadows drawn tight against his legs.

And Ivy realized with equal parts fear and tenderness that whatever the binding was doing to him it wasn't one-sided.

Chapter Twelve

Thorn was slower. It wasn't dramatic and anyone else might have missed it. But Ivy noticed the half-second delay when he reached for a box. The way his shoulders stayed tense while cutting ribbon. The faint dullness to his skin, the shadows beneath his eyes deepening like bruises.

By midmorning, she was sure that something was very wrong with him.

"You're sick or something," she said quietly as she passed him a bundle of ribbon.

"I am functioning," Thorn replied.

"You're lagging," she corrected.

He did not argue, which worried her more.

A woman with a sharp bob was at the counter, and she tilted her head toward Thorn. "Is your helper feeling alright, dear? He looks a bit under the weather."

"I'm fine," Thorn said automatically.

The woman frowned. "Mmm. He doesn't look it. The flu is going around. James down the street was in the hospital for three days because of it. Maybe you should take that one to urgent care."

Ivy forced a smile. "Long week."

The woman nodded sympathetically. "Tell him to eat something with substance. Maybe some chicken soup and bread."

Thorn inclined his head as if that settled it.

It didn't.

The delivery guy, Evan, arrived around noon, loud and familiar and entirely too energetic for Ivy's nerves. He leaned on the counter again, grin easy. "Big day soon," he said. "You holding up?"

"Barely," Ivy replied, focused on the register. "Tomorrow will be a circus. And the next day even worse."

His gaze flicked to Thorn who was standing farther away than usual, hands clasped tightly behind him.

"You alright, man?" Evan asked.

Thorn looked away. "Perfect."

"The vibe is off in this place today." Evan took a few pumps from the hand sanitizer next to the register. "Sickness is going around. Maybe it's time for some vitamins."

"Evan," Ivy slid four boxes across the counter, "these need to be delivered by noon."

"I'm on it." He took the boxes and left.

Lunch arrived shortly after. Two paper bags and a familiar smell filled the shop. Ivy glanced inside and blinked.

"Quesadillas?" she asked. "With extra sour cream?"

"You recommended them yesterday," Thorn said. "To the woman ordering sympathy flowers."

Her mouth fell open. "You remembered that?"

"Yes."

She stared at him as they sat at the counter to eat. He took a few careful bites, his gaze drifting back to her.

He looked hungry and pale.

She paused, quesadilla halfway to her mouth and she decided right then that enough was enough. She set her food down.

The moment the last customer left, Ivy flipped the sign to "Closed for Lunch" and locked the door with a decisive click.

"Thorn," she said, already moving.

"What?"

She grabbed his sleeve and dragged him toward the back before he could finish the sentence.

"What are you doing?" he asked.

"Something drastic," she said, hauling him into the stock room and slamming the door shut behind them. Buckets rattled. The single overhead bulb flickered on.

He straightened immediately, alarm flashing across his face. "Ivy, what are you doing?"

"Stop," she snapped. "Just stop." She turned on him, chest heaving. "You're not okay," she said. "You've been dragging ass all day. You're slower, weaker, and you look like hell."

"I am managing," Thorn said.

"No, you're not," Ivy shot back. "And Valentine's Day is just a few days away."

The words landed heavy.

"This isn't even the worst day yet," she continued. "If you can't keep up today, the shop will fail tomorrow and the next day. I will fail."

His jaw tightened. "I will endure."

"That's not good enough," she said fiercely. "I need you. I *need* your help."

The admission burned, raw and honest.

"You've been here all week," Ivy went on, voice breaking. "You've held this place together with me. And now you're just... fading." She stepped closer, lowering her voice. "Please," she said. "Let me do something for you."

Thorn shook his head. "No."

"Yes," she insisted. "You need blood. You've been starving yourself for days."

"I told you not to ask me that."

"I'm not asking," Ivy said. "I'm telling you. You're hurting yourself, and for what? Pride?"

"For safety," he snapped. "For you."

She laughed sharply, tears burning her eyes. "You think watching you fall apart is safer for me?"

Silence slammed into the room.

"Inviting you into my life was an accident," Ivy said. "But here you've been in my shop and in my home. You help me, you help this place, but you won't let me help you?"

The script beneath his skin flared faintly, agitated.

"I cannot," Thorn said, voice strained. "You do not understand the risk."

"Then explain it to me," she demanded. "Because from

where I'm standing, you're killing yourself slowly and calling it noble."

He looked away, breath shallow.

She reached for him, her fingertips on his jaw, forcing him to look at her. She remembered when they'd first touched and it hurt. It had changed over these past few days; so much had changed.

"Please," Ivy whispered. "Just this. Let me give you something back."

Thorn closed his eyes.

The room felt suddenly too small. The shadows stilled, drawn tight to his body.

"You are asking me," he said slowly, "to violate my restraint."

"I'm asking you to live," Ivy replied.

Another long silence.

"Yes." Thorn was quiet.

Ivy's breath caught. "Yes?"

Thorn opened his eyes, gaze dark and intent. "I will accept. On the condition that you understand this is not... simple."

Her pulse thundered. "I understand enough."

"No," he said gently. "You do not. But you are resolute."

He stepped closer, careful, controlled. "I will take only what is necessary," Thorn said. "No more."

Ivy nodded, heart racing, relief and fear tangling together.

"Okay," she whispered.

In the narrow stock room, Ivy Calder stood before a

Ledger Demon who had finally chosen need over law and the binding between them tightened, alive and listening.

Thorn did not rush and that alone made Ivy's breath hitch. He looked at her like she was a dessert about to be savored.

The stock room was close and warm, crowded with flowers and the quiet hum of the cooler beyond the wall. The air felt charged, like a storm caught between hits of lightning. Thorn stood before her, shadows drawn tight around his frame, restraint radiating from him like a held blade.

He took her arm, gently, raising it to his mouth. Dark eyes focused on hers.

"This will pinch," he warned.

Ivy swallowed hard and nodded. "It's okay."

Something in his expression shifted. Thorn's brows rose and a small smile showed his teeth. He inhaled against her skin then pressed his lips to the softness of her wrist. The contact was brief. Testing.

Suddenly, Ivy realized just how dangerous he was; not violent but seductive. Her body responded before her mind could catch up—thrumming, alive, caught between cool air and sudden heat. Her skin flushed as his mouth lingered and his breath ghosted over her pulse.

"Don't be afraid," Thorn whispered as his free arm wrapped around her waist and pulled her flush against his body. "I will not hurt you."

The closeness stole what little air she had left. She could feel the solid heat of him, the tension in his restraint, the way he held her like she was something precious.

"I... I'm not afraid." Ivy's eyes were wide as Thorn's

hand slid up her back, his thumb and fingers resting against the sharp edge of her ribcage as he held her steady.

His gaze searched her face, his eyes dark.

Only when she nodded again did he move.

The pinch was sharp and startling but fleeting, swallowed almost instantly by a flood of warmth. Thorn's breath stuttered against her skin, and Ivy felt the moment he gave in, the moment restraint yielded to need.

He fed carefully, not hurried or cruel like in the movies. She couldn't look away from where his lips moved against her skin.

Each pull sent a shiver through her, heat blooming low in her belly, her knees weakening as Thorn held her upright, anchoring her against his hard body. His grip tightened just enough to be sure she wouldn't fall, his mouth gentler than she'd imagined, the motion of his lips, his tongue against her skin: it made her insides melt.

The world narrowed to sensation and breath and the steady rhythm between them. Heat flooded her body and between her legs. Ivy sucked in a breath, she wasn't expecting that reaction. She didn't anticipate his feeding on her blood being a total turn on.

When Thorn finally pulled back, it was with visible effort. He pressed his forehead to hers, eyes closed, breathing hard as if he'd run a great distance. He licked his lips like he wanted more. His thumb brushed lightly over her wrist, soothing where his mouth had been, holding pressure to the puncture marks until they healed.

"Ivy," he said quietly, voice rough with control. "You should not have trusted me so completely."

She managed a soft, unsteady smile. "Too late."

For a long moment, they stayed held together in the dim light, the binding between them humming, undeniable and irrevocably *changed*.

AND THORN KNEW, WITH TERRIFYING CLARITY, that this was no longer just hunger. It was attachment. And the Ledger would never forgive it.

Chapter Thirteen

They didn't speak as they left the supply closet. Ivy adjusted her clothing as she walked to the front of the shop and unlocked the door. She forced a deep breath and tried to clear her mind and forget, like nothing extraordinary had just happened between buckets of ribbon and cardboard boxes.

The bell over the door chimed announcing more customers.

Thorn moved first.

It was subtle, but Ivy recognized color had come back to his skin, warmth blooming beneath the pale cast she'd grown used to over the last day. His eyes were sharper now, alert and focused, the hunger replaced by something grounded and controlled.

"Okay," Ivy said under her breath, relief loosening something in her chest. "There you are."

Thorn glanced at her, expression unreadable but calm. "I am restored."

She swallowed and nodded, turning back to the counter before she could stare too long.

The afternoon rush resumed with merciless efficiency.

Orders came in rapid-fire by way of walk-ins, phone calls, and online pickups. Ivy barely asked for help, but she didn't need to because Thorn was already there, anticipating, moving with precision that bordered on art. He trimmed stems cleanly, balanced arrangements instinctively, adjusted colors without being told.

Ivy watched him for half a second too long before catching herself.

A woman at the counter with a tailored coat and sharp eyes tilted her head as Thorn stepped forward with a finished bouquet.

"I'm sorry," she said politely, "but is your security guard making flower arrangements?"

Ivy didn't miss the faint amusement in her tone.

"Yes," Ivy replied smoothly. "He has a knack for it so I put him to work."

Thorn paused.

The woman raised a brow. "Does he now?"

"He does," Ivy said, taking the bouquet from Thorn and handing it over. "And he does a pretty good job."

The woman studied the arrangement, then smiled. "Well, I'll be damned. That's lovely."

She glanced at Thorn again, eyes flicking over his vest. "You know, if he's going to keep doing that, you might want to get him an apron. It's a bit hard to take flower advice from someone who looks like they're about to break kneecaps."

Ivy laughed. "Noted."

The woman left with a satisfied nod, bell jingling behind her.

Thorn looked down at the vest, then back at Ivy. "Is my appearance... disruptive?"

"Only a little," Ivy said lightly. "You do look intimidating."

He considered that. Then, without ceremony, he reached up and removed the security vest, setting it neatly under the counter. He unbuttoned the top few buttons of his shirt.

Ivy turned abruptly toward the back room. "I have an apron."

She returned moments later with a green apron she usually reserved for herself, soft from use, the tie strings long and familiar in her hands.

"Here," she said, holding it out.

Thorn took it. "Show me."

She stepped closer, fingers brushing his wrist as she adjusted the apron over his shoulders, reaching around his waist, wrapping the ties, her face entirely too close to his chest. Her hands lingered for half a second too long as she tied the apron.

When she stepped back, Thorn stood there still; shirt open just enough, sleeves rolled, apron settling against his frame like it belonged there. Like he'd always been there. Ivy swallowed hard. Damn. He looked... really good. Dangerous and domestic in equal measure. Like something out of place that somehow made everything else make sense.

Thorn tilted his head. "Is this acceptable?"

"Yes," she said, voice a little too quiet. "Very acceptable."

A corner of his mouth curved in not quite a smile, but close enough to make her pulse jump.

"Then I will continue," he said. "Without breaking kneecaps." This time, he flashed her a full smile and Ivy stopped breathing for a second. She'd never seen a soul so handsome.

Thorn turned back to the flowers, hands steady as he worked on the next order. The shop buzzed back to life around them but Ivy stood still for a moment, watching this impossible creature in her world, wearing her apron, saving her business one bouquet at a time.

She shook herself and reached for ribbon.

She had flowers to sell.

Chapter Fourteen

The burn came without warning.

Thorn was halfway through binding a bouquet of white roses and eucalyptus with a request for *forgiveness* written carefully on the order slip when the script beneath his skin ignited.

Pain tore through him, white-hot, as if the Ledger itself had seized him from the inside. His vision went black. The flowers slipped from his hands, stems striking the counter and scattering petals across the floor.

"Thorn?" Ivy said sharply.

He staggered back a step, breath tearing from his chest. The shadows around his feet recoiled, snapping inward as the script on his forearm burned brighter and angrier than Ivy had ever seen it.

Then the word appeared.

Just for a second.

Carved in searing red across his skin like a brand.

BREACH

Ivy froze and her stomach dropped through the floor.

"That…" Her voice shook. "That wasn't there before."

Thorn pressed his palm over the word, jaw clenched. The glow dimmed, but the damage had already been done.

"No," he said hoarsely.

She stepped closer, eyes locked on him. "What does that mean?"

For a long moment, Thorn didn't answer. Then he lowered his hand.

"The Ledger is no longer… aligned," he said carefully.

Ivy's heart pounded. "Aligned with what?"

"With me," Thorn replied.

He looked at the scattered flowers on the floor then at her. "Feeding from you crossed a threshold."

"I thought you said it was safe," she whispered, fingertips drifting over the faded mark where he'd bitten her.

"Something has changed," Thorn said. "Did I harm you?"

"No," Ivy shook her head.

"Did I frighten you? Or… something else." He shook his head then went still before asking, "Do you have feelings for me now?"

Ivy bit her lip and looked away, remembering the way her body had thrummed to life earlier when they were in the closet together. "I just met you," she said quietly. "I don't know what I'm feeling. I like you."

He turned his arm slightly so she could see where the script still pulsed faintly beneath his skin. "The Ledger recognizes intimacy as claim. Blood taken willingly, without breach, creates priority."

Her breath hitched. "Priority for… what?"

"For finalization," Thorn said quietly.

Ivy's knees went weak. She braced herself against the counter, mind scrambling to catch up.

"Finalize what?" she asked, though some part of her already knew.

"The contract," Thorn said. "All devotion clauses resolve on that day."

"And resolve means what exactly?" Her voice cracked.

He met her gaze, dark eyes unflinching now. Honest. "Either you are designated collateral," Thorn said, "bound permanently to the Ledger through me and Hell will take your soul...or I am reclaimed," he finished. "Stripped of function and erased."

The word echoed in the space between them. *Erased.*

Ivy shook her head slowly. "No. There has to be another option."

"There is not," Thorn said.

She laughed once, sharp and broken. "You're telling me that having feelings for you—"

"—has consequences," Thorn said.

Tears burned her eyes, furious and unwanted. "Then why didn't you say something to me? Why didn't you stop being so... so likeable? So nice? So protective and jealous and... you made me coffee and dinner and... How am I not supposed to develop feelings for you?"

His voice softened. "I did not want to reveal the cost."

She stepped forward, fists clenched at her sides, she felt gutted. "You should have told me it would cost you *everything.*"

"I am telling you now," he said quietly.

Outside, the world went on as cars passed and people walking by laughed, unaware that something ancient and terrible had just taken notice of a florist and a demon who dared to choose each other.

Ivy wiped her eyes angrily. "I won't let them erase you."

"You may not have a choice," Thorn said.

She looked at him.

She saw the man who wore her apron, who made her coffee, who protected her shop with his body and his will, and who had learned compassion because she demanded it.

And she understood, with brutal clarity, what loving him truly meant.

It wasn't safety.

It was defiance.

"Then we find a way," Ivy said fiercely. "Because I'm not handing over my soul and I'm not handing you over to Hell."

Something dangerous and bright stirred behind Thorn's eyes.

"The Ledger will not release me willingly," he warned.

Ivy stepped closer, close enough that she could feel the heat of him, the hum of the binding between them.

"Good," she said. "Neither will I."

AND SOMEWHERE DEEP WITHIN THORN'S SKIN THE Ledger pulsed again, no longer certain it was in control.

Chapter Fifteen

Thorn turned the shop sign to "Closed." It was dark outside and the streetlamps had flickered on nearly an hour ago.

She crossed the open space to Thorn.

"Tell me," she said. "What does Hell actually lose if you defect?"

Thorn did not answer immediately and that frightened her.

He wandered for a moment, stopping near the worktable, hands resting on the scarred wood as if grounding himself. The script beneath his skin glowed faintly. It was no longer flaring like a system under strain.

"Ledger Demons are rare," he said at last.

"How rare?" Ivy pressed.

"There are fewer than a hundred," Thorn replied. "The throne keeps close track of us."

"That's it?"

"Yes."

"And you're... what?" she asked. "Middle management?"

Something like a smile touched his mouth but it was brief and humorless.

"I am primary enforcement," Thorn said. "I specialize in high-risk contracts. Soul collection. Sovereignty. Bloodline obligation."

Ivy's stomach dropped. "Definitely not middle management."

"No," Thorn said. "I am a weapon."

The word landed hard between them.

"If I defect," he continued calmly, "contract law destabilizes. Claims fail. Enforcement weakens. Hell loses souls. And souls are power to the throne."

She stared at him. "You're telling me the infernal economy depends on you staying in line. You're like the mafia, collecting souls for them."

"Ledger Demons must remain obedient," Thorn corrected. "And yes. Souls are currency."

Ivy let out a shaky laugh. "But I made a mistake. I wasn't some slimy slum lord calling a demon to fix my bank account."

Thorn shrugged. "That's accurate. The sitting Prince might let your Ledger go."

"So Hell doesn't want me."

"No," Thorn said. "Hell wants me."

The realization cracked something open in her chest. All this time she'd been thinking of herself as the risk. The collateral. The fragile human who might be crushed beneath Hell's attention.

But Thorn... Thorn was the prize. Hell wanted to keep him, forever.

She stepped closer, voice low. "Then I won't let you be destroyed for me. I won't allow it," she said. "I won't be the reason Hell erases you. I'll release you. Take my soul now. We'll void the contract, whatever it takes. I've tried to once already; whatever constructs are running this getup shouldn't be surprised."

"No," Thorn said immediately. "It doesn't work like that."

She flinched. "You don't get to decide that alone."

"I do," he replied. "Because this is my existence. I am not of the mortal realm."

She shook her head, tears threatening again. "You think I can live with that? Knowing you were taken away because you stayed?"

"I stayed because I chose to," Thorn said.

"You stayed because you were bound by the Ledger!"

His voice sharpened. "Not entirely." He stepped toward her, closing the distance until the air between them felt charged and alive. "I stayed because I wanted to," Thorn said. "It was a test. A... curiosity."

Ivy froze.

"I was empty before you," Thorn said, voice steady but raw beneath the restraint. "I enforced. I corrected. I erased. There was no difference between one moment and the next."

His gaze held hers, unblinking.

"That was not living," she said.

Her throat tightened.

"You gave me perspective," he continued. "Choice.

Resistance. You made me see consequence as something other than punishment. Ivy," he said, her name heavy on his tongue. "If Hell erases me, it will not be because of you. It will be because I refused to return to emptiness. I am tired. I wanted this experience. From the moment I saw you that first night. I wanted to stay."

Tears slipped free, hot and silent as Ivy reached for him, fingers curling into the front of his shirt. "I don't want to be the thing that costs you everything."

"You are the thing that gave me something," Thorn said quietly. "For the first time."

The Ledger pulsed sharply beneath his skin—a warning—but he did not look away.

"If I must choose between annihilation and obedience," Thorn said, voice dark, "I choose defiance."

Ivy pressed her forehead to his chest, breath shaking. "You're so stupid." She slammed her fists against his chest. "Defiance is not annihilation or obedience. You're mixing up words."

Thorn's hand came up, resting between her shoulders.

"Yes," he said. "Perhaps erasure is already taking place."

Chapter Sixteen

One Day until Valentine's Day

The shop should have been chaos. It should have broken under the weight of last-minute orders and frantic hearts but instead it moved with an almost eerie precision. Ivy barely had time to think. Flowers flowed through her hands in a steady rhythm, arrangements forming faster than she could remember making them.

And they were... different.

Roses opened wider than they should have. Tulips unfurled hours ahead of schedule. Greens stayed vivid, resilient, as if refusing to wilt no matter how many times they were trimmed.

Ivy felt it every time she crossed the threshold behind the counter. The shop hummed softly as a low, steady presence beneath the noise like a promise woven into the walls. It was the contract protecting its asset.

Thorn was focused and efficient. He moved through the space like it belonged to him, hands quick and sure, gaze constantly tracking the room. Nothing spilled. Nothing broke. No one raised their voice. Even the most frantic customers softened when they stepped inside, shoulders easing as if they'd crossed into a different world.

People lingered. They stopped to talk to Ivy and Thorn. That never happened on Valentine's Eve before; usually everyone was in such a rush.

A woman picking up a dozen red roses paused near the door, bouquet tucked under her arm. She glanced around the shop with a puzzled smile.

"It's strange," she said. "This place feels really safe right now. I think I'll come back tomorrow. I like the vibe."

Ivy's hands stilled.

Thorn's gaze flicked to her.

The woman laughed lightly, embarrassed by her own words. "That probably sounds silly."

"No," Ivy said quietly. "It doesn't."

The woman nodded once, satisfied, and left.

The bell chimed.

By the time Ivy locked the door that night, her body felt wrung out but the shop stood pristine, glowing softly beneath the lights. Orders were stacked and labeled. Deliveries lined up for dawn. Not a single flower sagged. And Evan had agreed to be there at nine a.m. sharp to start delivering all the orders.

Ivy leaned against the counter and exhaled.

"We did it," she murmured.

"For now," Thorn said.

She looked up at him, something tightening in her chest. "That sounded like a goodbye."

His expression didn't change but the shadows at his feet stirred.

"I need to show you something," he said.

The way he said it sent a chill through her.

They went upstairs in silence.

The apartment felt smaller than it had hours before, the walls pressing in as if they knew something bad was coming. Ivy barely had time to set her bag down before Thorn stiffened.

"Ivy," he said sharply.

She crossed the room just as the air shifted.

Thorn gasped as light tore through his shirt and a rune burned itself into his chest, lines of infernal script carving deep and bright. He staggered, bracing himself against the counter as the mark flared violently, heat rolling off him in waves.

"No," Ivy whispered, panic flooding her. "No, no, no..." She moved closer to him.

"This is the summons from the throne," Thorn said through clenched teeth. "Formal."

The rune pulsed once, twice, and then settled into a steady, ominous glow.

Ivy reached for him, stopping just short of touching the mark. "What does that mean?"

He lifted his head.

"Hell is done asking," Thorn said. "They will reclaim me soon."

Her chest seized. "Reclaim how?"

"The Ledger will finalize the contract. One way or

another."

She swallowed hard. "You said there were two options."

"Yes."

Her voice shook. "Say them again."

Thorn met her gaze, unwavering.

"Either you are bound as collateral and your soul collected," he said, "or I am erased."

Silence slammed into the room.

Outside, the world slept. Somewhere below them, the shop rested—full, alive, impossibly safe.

Ivy's hands curled into fists.

"You have until dawn," she said.

"Yes."

She stepped closer, close enough to feel the heat of the rune, the truth of it burning into both of them.

"I want you to stay," Ivy said honestly.

A dangerous light flickered behind Thorn's eyes. "I can tell."

Ivy paced the apartment. She went to the kitchen and opened a bottle of wine then poured two glasses.

She drank hers all in one gulp then rubbed her face.

Thorn moved closer before picking up his glass. "I don't think this will help."

Ivy shook her head. "I don't know anything about your world or Hell. I have no idea how to stop you from leaving, how to stop them from taking you."

She was shaking her head in disbelief and holding back tears that were burning her eyes.

"To surviving Valentine's Eve," she said, raising her refilled glass.

Thorn lifted his glass. "To endurance."

They drank.

The wine warmed her chest, softened the sharp edges of fear she'd been holding at bay since the rune burned into him moments ago. Ivy leaned back against the counter, studying him. She didn't like the faint glow beneath his skin, the tension in his shoulders, and the way he looked like he was already halfway gone.

"I couldn't have done this week without you," she said quietly. "And I'm afraid you'll never understand just how much that means to me." The words slipped out before she could stop them. The wine was loosening her lips. She set her glass down and laughed softly, shaking her head. "This is ridiculous."

"What is?" Thorn asked.

She exhaled, the truth heavy and unavoidable. She'd had one night stands before; this was nothing, he'd be leaving soon, he'd go away and she'd be alone again... she saddened at the thought. Maybe she would keep her soul but suddenly she wasn't sure if it was worth it.

The thought surprised her.

"Ivy," he said gently.

She didn't look up.

"Ivy," he touched her chin and lifted her gaze to meet his. "Are you ill?"

Her breath caught.

"No," she whispered. "I'm just... sad."

She rose onto her tiptoes before doubt could stop her and pressed her lips to his. He was warm and tasted like mint and wine.

For a heartbeat Thorn froze, then his hands came up,

steady and careful, as if she were something precious he didn't yet trust himself to hold.

Ivy pressed herself against him, hands sliding over his shoulders, up the back of his neck and into his hair.

The contact was electric.

Thorn exhaled against her mouth, a low sound torn from him, and deepened the kiss just enough to tell her he felt it too. The shadows stirred, not in warning but in awe.

When they finally pulled apart, foreheads resting together, the air between them felt charged.

"We need to think," Ivy murmured. "There has to be a way around the Ledger. Systems have flaws. Every system does."

"Yes," Thorn agreed, voice rough. "They rely on authority."

"And authority can be challenged," she said.

His hands tightened slightly at her waist. "You are not afraid."

She smiled sadly. "I am."

Thorn brushed his thumb along her jaw, reverent. "If there is a way," he said quietly, "it will cost me everything."

Ivy met his gaze without flinching. "Then we make it worth it."

He kissed her again, slower this time, deeper, a promise pressed to her lips.

Hell had already lost its advantage because Thorn no longer wanted to belong. And Ivy would not let him go.

"The other day you mentioned a Blood bond." Ivy was running her fingers along the seam of his shirt. "Tell me about that."

His body went still. "Don't…"

She held up a finger. "Actually you said, Blood rituals are as old as time. Angels, demons, and gods have all consumed blood to survive. Some have strayed from the practice, but in Hell, it's how we survive. For some, the blood bonds them for life and they cannot live without each other." Her eyes searched his. "You've tasted my blood once already and ever since then I haven't been right. I keep staring at you. Watching you. Thinking about you." She reached for the buttons of his shirt and started undoing them. "I think you were onto something there. If we are bonded then your employer can't risk both of our deaths, can they?"

Thorn grabbed her, palms against her face holding her gaze to his. "You do not know what you ask. A Blood bond is serious."

She pulled his shirt until the buttons popped off. "My shop is serious. Selling those god damned flowers is serious." She pulled his shirt loose from his pants. "Everything here is as serious as a heart attack. If your kind only take blood rituals seriously, then I'm about to give them one."

He released her face and that seemed to set her off. Ivy shoved his chest, pushing him backward, toward the bedroom.

"I don't think you know what you're getting yourself into," Thorn warned.

"I'm ready for it."

He fell backward onto the bed.

Ivy was tearing off her clothes. Her sweater was on the floor, she kicked off her shoes and they hit hard against the wall. She reached for the button of her jeans but Thorn's large hands stopped her.

"You cannot force a Blood bond," he warned. "And this is not something you can ever walk away from."

"What makes you think I'd do such a thing?" She shucked her jeans off and tossed them. "Now," she said, moving close and standing between his legs, "tell me about the Blood bond. Do we cut our palms and shake on it?"

"Why would we do that in our underwear?" he asked.

Ivy blushed all the way down to her belly button. "Well I just... assumed. After you fed from me yesterday I felt kind of..." She licked her lips.

Thorn smiled. "You liked it."

"Yeah," she reached for his shoulders. "I liked it."

Thorn grabbed her hips and pulled her close, then yanked her down onto his lap and kissed her.

Ivy leaned into him. She knew he'd kiss like this after she'd watched his mouth on her wrist. Firm and soft. When his tongue pierced through her lips she let him in. He gripped her body harder as he kissed her again and again and again until she was breathless.

Ivy finally pulled away, breathing heavy. "Is there more?"

He nodded slowly, showing his sharp teeth. "I will drink your blood. And you will drink mine."

"Then what happens?" She touched her mouth. "Oh, wait, I don't have sharp teeth like you."

"I'll help you with that."

"Okay, but what happens after we drink from each other?"

"Does it frighten you?" he asked. "I am a demon, after all. Would you like to change your mind?" he offered.

"Because now that you've given your blood and your mouth, I'm finding it very hard to restrain myself."

She reached up, fingertips drifting across his shoulders before threading into his hair. "I'm not changing my mind. I'm not losing the shop or you."

Ivy straddled his lap and Thorn reached behind them. "Now the blood," he warned, holding a small knife. He held it against his hand and drew blood. "For you," his words were soft. "Once this happens, you don't get to ask me to stop."

"And you?" she asked, licking her lips.

"Here," his hand touched the side of her throat. "We consume the blood together."

"Okay." She nodded. She felt his mouth on her skin, the warmth of his lips then his tongue, then the sharp bite.

Warmth flooded Ivy's body and her vision blurred. She glanced to the blood in his hand and leaned forward, pressing her lips to it.

Thorn groaned.

Something snapped tight in Ivy's chest when she swallowed his blood down. It tasted like wine, sweet and dry. She pulled away, feeling high.

Thorn caught her before she fell off his lap, pressing his forehead to hers, breath ragged.

"It's done," he whispered.

Her voice came out steady anyway. "Did it work?"

A pause.

Then, grimly, "Yes."

"And the cost?"

His jaw tightened. "Hell will come."

Ivy swallowed, still tasting him, still feeling the bond humming violently beneath her skin.

"Good," she said. "Then they'll have to deal with both of us."

Behind Thorn's eyes, something ancient and feral lit. Defiance.

And somewhere beyond the Veil, the Ledger registered a catastrophic error it had no protocol to correct.

Chapter Seventeen

The runes burned again. Thorn stiffened, breath locking in his chest as the mark on his skin flared and pulled like a hook meant to drag him out of the room.

But the light sputtered and faded, then tried again.

Thorn stared down at his chest.

"What?" Ivy asked, already bracing herself.

"A summons," Thorn said slowly. "The authorization is absolute."

The rune flared once more.

Then nothing.

The lights dimmed and three shapes unfolded out of the shadows near the far wall.

Ledger Demons.

Their script moved beneath their skin like ink suspended in water.

One stepped forward.

"Thorn," it said. "You have been summoned to explain."

Thorn straightened. "I was summoned already," he said. "The rune failed."

"Yes," the demon replied. "That is why we are here."

Ivy stepped closer, instinctively reaching for Thorn's arm. "You don't get to just burst in out of thin air and make demands."

The second demon turned its gaze on her.

Ivy froze.

"You are not named in this summons," the demon said calmly.

Ivy swallowed. "Leave him alone."

The first demon looked at her again. "This is not a collection," it said. "It is an inquiry."

Thorn's jaw tightened. "You want an explanation."

"Yes," the demon said. "The Throne requires clarification regarding a failed summons, a corrupted rune, and an unregistered refusal."

Ivy's breath hitched.

Unregistered.

The third demon spoke for the first time.

"You are to present yourself," it said to Thorn, "and explain what has occurred."

Thorn didn't move.

"And if I refuse?" he asked.

The first demon regarded him evenly.

"Then the Throne will determine whether refusal still applies. Or erasure."

Ivy felt cold crawl up her spine.

Thorn looked down at her.

For a moment, the apartment felt unbearably small.

"They are not here for you," he said quietly.

Her fingers tightened in his shirt. "That doesn't make this better."

"No," Thorn agreed. "It makes it worse."

He turned back to the demons.

"I will go," he said.

Ivy's heart dropped. "Thorn, don't."

He leaned down, pressing his forehead briefly to hers.

Her voice shook. "You're coming back."

Something unreadable flickered across his face.

"Yes," he said. "One way or another."

The demons stepped closer.

"Do not touch her," Thorn said sharply.

The first demon inclined its head. "She is claimed."

They opened a rift in the air, a precise incision, clean as a ledger line drawn straight through reality.

Thorn stepped into it without resistance.

The rift closed behind him.

The apartment fell silent.

Ivy stood alone in the dim light, the smell of flowers still lingering in the air, the bed still warm where Thorn had been moments before.

Ivy understood with terrifying clarity that being left behind was not mercy.

It was leverage.

"She is claimed." Repeated over and over again in Ivy's mind.

Chapter Eighteen

Thorn was escorted through corridors of stone. The demons did not restrain him. They did not need to. There were enough Hellions guarding the Castle in the Burning Caves that he'd never make it out alive if he ignored the summons and tried to run. Their presence pressed in from all sides; silent and armored, wings folded tight against their backs. The Hellions were warriors; if he ran there would be an execution, not a negotiation.

The halls were carved from obsidian and stone. At the end of the corridor was an office.

Thorn slowed, unease threading through him for the first time since the summons had burned into his chest.

Thorn straightened his back, ready to face the Queen of Hell. The door opened and Thorn was greeted not by the Queen but by a princeling. Remington.

He stood behind a massive desk cluttered with papers, ledgers stacked in careful disorder, a map of the realms pinned to the stone wall behind him. He looked young by Hell's standards. He was young and dark-haired, sharp-eyed, dressed not in armor but in tailored black, sleeves rolled as if he'd been working for hours.

Which, Thorn realized, he probably had.

Remington was the son of Meg, Queen of Hell, and Sparrow, the Raven King, and born of a love that defied Heaven, Hell, and every system designed to prevent it. His very existence was evidence that bonds formed by choice, not decree, could outlast the laws of Hell. And that made him far more dangerous than the Queen.

Thorn bowed.

"Come sit," the princeling ordered, pointing to a chair.

Thorn obeyed.

Remington did not sit. He leaned a hip against the desk, arms crossed, studying Thorn with open curiosity rather than hostility.

"You know," Remington said conversationally, "most Ledger Demons don't make it this far once they're flagged."

Thorn kept his gaze level. "I assume my classification delayed erasure."

"Yes," Remington agreed. "High-value enforcement Ledger Demons get... reviews." He tilted his head. "You're very expensive, Thorn."

Thorn said nothing.

Remington sighed and pushed off the desk, finally taking his seat. He opened a book that was thick and scarred with annotations.

"Let's start simple," Remington said. "You were summoned to the mortal realm to assist a flower shop owner." Remington glanced up. "Ivy Calder. The agreement was signed. Her shop's success for her soul. Why did the Ledger fail?"

Thorn answered without hesitation. "Because I was compromised."

A pause.

Remington's brow lifted slightly. "That part we caught. What I'm asking is *why* the refusal held."

Thorn felt the cracked heat of the Ledger beneath his skin respond, restless but silent.

"Because my alignment has changed," Thorn said.

Remington tapped a finger against the page. "That's not an answer. That's a symptom."

Thorn's jaw tightened.

"You fed," Remington said calmly.

"Yes."

"On a mortal."

"Yes."

"Without coercion."

There was a pause. "Yes."

Remington closed the book softly. "That's where things get interesting." He leaned back in his chair, gaze sharpening. "Ledger Demons feed all the time. That alone doesn't compromise summons authority."

Thorn inhaled once. Steady. Controlled.

"I chose to feed," he said. "I chose the source. I chose restraint. And I chose to remain afterward."

Remington's eyes flicked briefly in interest.

"And you developed attachment," he said.

"Yes."

"Want."

"Yes."

"Priority deviation."

"Yes."

Each admission stacked neatly between them, like evidence laid out for a verdict.

Remington exhaled slowly. "You realize," he said, "that from the throne's perspective, you didn't malfunction."

Thorn frowned.

"You evolved," Remington continued. "And systems hate that."

Silence stretched.

He cleared his throat. "The mortal," Remington said at last. "Ivy Calder."

Thorn's shoulders went rigid. "She's not collateral," Thorn said immediately. "She is not bound. The ledger did not hold."

"I know," Remington interrupted, holding up a hand. "Relax. If Hell wanted her soul, this conversation would be happening very differently."

That did not reassure Thorn nearly as much as Remington seemed to think it should.

Remington studied him for a long moment. "You care about her."

"Yes."

"You would choose her over function."

"Yes."

"You would choose her over Hell."

Thorn did not hesitate. "Yes."

That earned a quiet laugh.

Remington shook his head, something like admiration flickering across his face. "You know," he said softly, "my parents did something like that."

Thorn's gaze snapped to him.

"That's not a threat," Remington added. "It's context."

He stood and moved around the desk, stopping a few feet from Thorn. "Here's the problem," Remington said. "The Ledger doesn't know what to do with you anymore. You're registered as property. As enforcement. As law. And yet," he continued, "you've demonstrated autonomy."

Thorn said nothing.

"That deviates from your job," Remington said frankly. "Your job requires violence, always has. But you're *selective* now. You cannot be trusted to perform as usual."

He met Thorn's eyes.

"What happens next?" Thorn asked.

Remington's expression sobered.

"We need some kind of resolution," he said. "Get back in alignment. Or be removed."

"And Ivy?"

Remington's mouth tightened. "She's leverage. Not because Hell wants her but because Hell knows *you* do. You'll have to figure something out to protect her."

Thorn stood abruptly. "You will not touch her."

"Sit," Remington snapped and shadows burst from his body in threat.

Thorn froze, then sat.

Remington exhaled. "I'm not my mother," he said quietly. "I don't rule by terror. But I do rule." He leaned forward. "You have until..." he looked down at the calendar in front of him. "Hm. Look at that. Valentine's day. I'll give you one day after."

Thorn swallowed. "To do what?"

"To decide," Remington said. "Whether you return to your duties... or force the system to acknowledge something it was never designed to allow. Which might be the end of Ledger Demons. You could free your kind."

Remington held his gaze, unflinching.

"You'll need to do something no Ledger Demon has ever done," he said. "Make your Ledger uncollectable."

"How?" Thorn asked.

Remington straightened. "That," he said, "is your problem. I've got enough on my plate."

The door behind Thorn opened.

The Hellions waited, silent.

As Thorn was escorted away, Remington spoke once more—quiet, almost thoughtful. "For what it's worth," he said, "I hope you succeed."

Thorn did not look back.

Chapter Nineteen

Ivy was staring at the contract, memories flooding her mind as she tried to think of a way out of this mess.

In exchange for relief from burdens of the business Calder Floral, the undersigned offers binding of their corporeal soul, enforceable upon the Ledger's judgement.

Ivy recounted the memory, the torn halves of the contract flaring white-hot in her hands. The pieces hitting the counter and fusing back together. The ink of Ivy's signature pulsing.

The script beneath Thorn's skin had flared bright as lines of red threaded up his throat.

"That was unwise."

"What was that?"

"The contract is malformed now."

"Malformed?"

"It bound improperly."

"I don't know what that means. You talk weird."

"It means that the binding reached for the nearest eligible anchor."

"Which was...?"

"Me."

"No. No, that's not possible. This is nuts. What happens now?"

"I cannot leave. The contract tethers me to the point of summoning."

SHE'D ASKED FOR HELP AND THEN BOUND HIM TO this place. Ivy swallowed hard and looked out the front windows of the shop. It was dark out, nearly midnight. She couldn't stand in the empty apartment staring at the wall where the world stretched apart and he'd been taken away.

Ivy sighed, the agreement under her fingertips. She flicked the edge of the paper, wondering if she should rip it again.

"No," she murmured. "I'm not making it worse."

She turned off the lights, locked the door out of habit—once, twice, a third time—and climbed the narrow stairs to the apartment above.

The space felt empty without him. It was strange, he'd only been there barely a week but she missed him.

Ivy showered and changed into pajamas. Her movements were slow and heavy. She brushed her teeth, washed her face, and stared at her reflection longer than necessary. Her eyes looked tired. Red-rimmed. There was a faint flush along her throat she hadn't noticed earlier. She touched it and her skin felt warm.

"That figures," she muttered. "I'm barely through the busiest week of the year and now I'm getting sick."

The thought made her stomach sink; Valentine's Day morning and she needed to be in tip-top shape. Deliveries, walk-ins, emergencies, mistakes that couldn't be undone. There was no room for a fever. No margin for weakness.

She crawled into bed and turned onto her side, pulling the blankets tight around her shoulders. Sleep did not come easily.

When it did, she dreamed of red ink spreading across white paper. Of flowers blooming too fast, their petals dark and slick. Of shadows pooling at the foot of her bed, unmoving, waiting.

She woke with a start. Her throat ached. Ivy swallowed and winced.

"Great," she whispered hoarsely. "Fantastic. Love that for me. Illness on the biggest day of the year. I hope I don't have the flu." Thorn's kisses flashed through her mind. "I hope he didn't have some Hell-flu."

She rolled onto her back and stared at the ceiling, heart beating a little too fast. Her pulse felt loud in her ears. She pressed her fingers lightly to her neck and paused.

Her skin was warm there. She closed her eyes again. Sleep came in fragments after that. She woke often. Checked the time. Shifted positions. Thought about the shop. About Thorn. About the way he'd looked at her the last time she'd seen him.

By the time her alarm went off, Ivy felt like she'd barely slept at all. She got up, got dressed, twisted her hair up in a bun, and made tea hoping it would soothe her throat.

Valentine's Day had arrived.

Ivy gave herself a little pep talk. "You've got this. You've done this for eight years. This year is no different. You've always been alone."

Chapter Twenty

By the time Ivy reached the bottom of the stairs, there were already people outside the shop. Through the front window she saw dark shapes bundled in coats, stamping their feet against the snow, shoulders hunched against the cold. A small line stretched past the neighboring storefront, breath fogging in pale bursts as they shifted impatiently.

Someone knocked. Not gently.

Ivy paused at the door, keys heavy in her hand.

"It's eight," a muffled voice called through the glass. "Your hours say eight."

"I know," Ivy muttered, unlocking the deadbolt. The bell rang as she opened the door and cold air rushed in.

"About time," someone muttered.

Another voice followed. "I've been standing out here for fifteen minutes."

"It's snowing," someone else complained. "You'd think they'd open early today of all days."

Ivy stepped aside and let them funnel in, face neutral, spine straight. She didn't apologize. She didn't explain. She flipped the sign to "Open," and moved on instinct.

She crossed behind the counter and reached for her apron, then stopped. Thorn's apron still hung over the back of the chair. For half a second, the world narrowed to that stupid piece of fabric and the way her throat tightened like it might close entirely.

She swallowed hard.

Not now.

Ivy took her own apron from the hook, tied it quickly, and turned her back on the chair.

The first customer was already at the counter.

"I need two dozen red roses," a man said briskly. "Delivery before noon."

Ivy nodded. "Name?"

She wrote it all down, rang up the order and handed him the receipt, then moved on. That was the trick. Keep moving.

Orders stacked fast. Names, addresses, and love notes scribbled in cramped handwriting. The bell rang again and again, the line refusing to shrink. Phones started ringing. Online orders pinged in steady, merciless intervals.

She didn't think.

She *worked*.

By the time she finished the fifteenth order, her head was buzzing and her throat burned every time she swallowed. She took a quick sip of the now cold tea, ignored the ache, and kept going.

"I need something impressive for my boss," a woman said breathlessly. "Like... save-my-marriage impressive."

"Roses or lilies?" Ivy asked.

"Both."

Of course. Ivy showed the woman a picture of a massive bouquet.

"Yes." The woman nodded. "I'll take ten of those. Can you deliver before dinner?"

Ivy's face went pale. "Of course," she promised.

Evan showed up, shaking snow from his jacket, grin already in place.

"Well," he said, glancing at the business of the shop, "looks like Cupid threw up in here."

Ivy slid a delivery manifest across the counter without looking at him. "Good morning, Evan."

"Morning to you too," he added, undeterred. "You look—"

"Hudson Street first," Ivy said flatly. "Then Elm, then the hotel downtown. Fifty arrangements total for the Prescott order. They need to be out by ten-thirty."

Evan blinked. "Fifty?"

"Yes."

"Is your..." He hesitated, eyes flicking instinctively toward the space Thorn usually occupied. "Is your security guy around today?"

Ivy didn't look up. "No."

"Oh," Evan said, the joke faltering. "Uh. Okay then. Guess it's just us today. We got this."

She didn't respond.

He cleared his throat. "Right. Boxes?"

"By the cooler. Make sure you come back immediately," she waved a receipt at him. "This next delivery is going to be giant."

Evan nodded and moved quickly. He pulled on a pair of gloves, loaded up his cart and headed for the delivery truck.

Ivy exhaled through her nose and turned toward the worktable.

Fifty arrangements.

Special order. Identical. White roses, blush ranunculus, eucalyptus, silver ribbon. She lined them up with ruthless efficiency, hands moving on muscle memory alone. Strip. Cut. Arrange. Wrap. Repeat.

Her wrists ached. Her throat burned. Sweat prickled at her spine despite the cold.

The phone rang. She paused to answer it.

Another large order of twenty bouquets of roses. "I'll have it to you by dinner," she promised as she processed the order and charged their credit card.

Ivy paused for just a moment to glance at the total sales for the day and her eyes went wide. Fifteen-thousand and she'd only been open a few hours.

She got back to work and did not stop. She did not look at the chair behind the counter. She did not think about the way Thorn used to stand beside her during mornings like this all silent and steady and anticipating what she needed before she asked.

She did not think about Hell.

She did not think about the contract.

She made bouquets and arrangements.

By eleven o'clock, the shop was humming like a live

wire. Customers pressed close, voices overlapping, impatience sharp and frantic. Someone complained about the wait time. Someone else demanded a refund. Someone cried at the counter over a card they didn't know how to word.

Ivy talked the refund complaint into store credit. She passed a laminated page with pre-written notes to the man whining about not knowing what to write on their card.

Her throat throbbed. Her head felt light. She ignored it.

As she tied the ribbon on the fifteenth identical bouquet, Ivy's fingers slipped for just a second, and she hit a thorn and sliced her finger. The bow came out crooked. She stared at it, breath shallow.

Blood dripped on the counter and the floor. She grabbed a towel to wipe it away and as she crouched behind the counter, searching for a bandage, she found another drop of blood on embossed paper. The contract.

A dozen more online orders pinged and the phone buzzed.

Tension filled Ivy's chest. She suddenly felt completely overwhelmed.

She bandaged her finger, stood, and took a deep breath. She had to keep it together; this day could not fall apart. She'd never dig herself out of the negative reviews or chargebacks if it all fell apart. She could do this. She had to do this.

She fixed the bow and set it straight. Then wrapped up the order in brown craft paper, taped it and stacked the bouquets in a delivery box.

Ivy grabbed the online orders off the printer. Her stomach growled and she immediately regretted skipping breakfast. She should have been thrilled about the thirty orders that had just come in from her website but as she added them to the stack of orders waiting to be prepared, dread filled her.

The door dinged and Ivy looked down at her bandaged finger.

"Excuse me." His voice was measured, calm, expensive.

She glanced up.

The man standing at the counter didn't look like her usual Valentine's Day crowd. No snow-dusted desperation. No crumpled card in his hand. He wore a tailored coat, scarf draped just so, watch gleaming at his wrist.

"Yes?" Ivy asked.

"I'm looking for Ivy Calder," he said. "Owner."

"That's me."

Relief crossed his face. "Thank God," he said, exhaling. "I'm Don, from Bella Napoli. Our florist canceled this morning. Burst pipe, I think. Or a breakdown. I didn't ask." He waved a hand. "I was told you might be able to help."

Ivy's pulse kicked up. "What do you need?"

He leaned in slightly, lowering his voice as if the number itself were obscene.

"Two hundred table centerpieces," he said. "Low arrangements. Elegant. Whites and reds. Nothing overpowering. And fifty bouquets for VIP tables and private rooms."

The shop seemed to tilt.

"Today?" Ivy asked, even though she already knew the answer.

"Yes." He glanced at his watch. "The dining room opens in four hours."

Four.

Hours.

Ivy's mind raced. Buckets. Stems. Ribbon. Labor. Deliveries already scheduled. Her hands started to sweat.

"I..." She swallowed. "That's a very large order."

"I know." He nodded, earnest. "And I wouldn't ask if I had another option. But if you can do this, I will never use another florist again. Weekly arrangements. Events. Holidays. Everything. They're yours."

Her accountant's voice whispered faintly in the back of her skull, "*This is when you make it.*"

She forced herself to breathe.

"I can do it," Ivy said with a smile.

The words came out before fear could stop them.

The man's shoulders sagged with relief. "You're a miracle worker."

"Let's not get ahead of ourselves," she said, already reaching for the order pad. "I'll need specifics. Table count. Vase preferences. Delivery windows."

He answered everything quickly, like a man who lived in logistics.

When she finished tallying the total, her breath caught just slightly. It was way more than she made in a good Valentine's month.

She slid the receipt across the counter.

He didn't blink. He simply paid in full.

He slid his card at the reader. It flashed approved.

His signature was neat and he even added a twenty percent tip.

"Thank you," he said sincerely, clasping her hand for just a second. "You've saved my Valentine's Day."

"You're welcome," Ivy managed.

"I'll have my manager call you tomorrow to set up ongoing service," he added, already backing toward the door. "We take care of people who take care of us."

She smiled. She even waved as he left. As the bell chimed, Ivy turned and looked at the coolers. Her stomach dropped.

Roses were dwindling fast, the reds especially. Whites nearly gone. She stepped closer, counting automatically, heart starting to race.

No. No, no, no.

Two hundred centerpieces.

Fifty bouquets.

Plus the online orders.

And she was already running on fumes.

The phone chirped.

She ignored it.

The bell rang again.

"Excuse me," someone said sharply. "I've been waiting."

"I'll be right with you," Ivy said, voice tight.

Another order pinged in online.

Her chest felt too small for her lungs. She tightened the knot of her apron with shaking fingers, nails biting into the fabric.

You can do this, she told herself fiercely. *You have to.*

But as she stared into the cooler, calculating loss faster than hope, panic crept up her spine like ice water.

Thorn would have noticed already.

He would have moved.

He would have *fixed* something.

Ivy squeezed her eyes shut for half a second, then opened them and straightened.

The line waited.

The phone rang.

And she stepped behind the counter, smiling through the fracture spreading quietly through her chest.

The door chimed again and Ivy was afraid to look up.

Chapter Twenty-One

The phone was now ringing without mercy. A woman at the counter sighed loudly.

"I'll be right with you," Ivy said for what felt like the hundredth time, her hands shaking. Her throat ached. Her head throbbed. The massive restaurant order loomed like a guillotine in the back of her mind, ticking down by the second.

She turned to grab another bundle of greenery and froze. Someone stood just inside the door. Tall. Still. Dark coat dusted with snow. For one awful heartbeat, Ivy thought her exhaustion had finally cracked her. Her vision swam.

No, she thought. *No, don't do this to me. Not now.*

The man took a step forward. The shadows at his feet settled like they recognized where they belonged. Of course they did, he was bound to this place.

Ivy's breath left her in a sound that wasn't quite a sob.

"Thorn," she whispered.

He didn't look surprised to see her. He looked...

committed. He crossed the shop without hurry, as if the chaos bent instinctively around him. Customers faltered mid-complaint. The air shifted, pressure easing in his wake. He stopped at the counter.

Ivy stared at him, unable to move, unable to breathe.

"You're..." Her voice cracked. "You came back."

"I know," Thorn said calmly.

Her hands fisted in her apron. "I'm hallucinating."

"You are not," he replied.

The phone rang again. Someone cleared their throat pointedly.

Thorn glanced around the shop once, taking everything in with frightening speed. The line, the order slips, the near-empty cooler, the way Ivy looked like she might collapse if someone breathed too hard in her direction, he saw it all.

Then, without asking, he shrugged out of his coat and tossed it over the back of a chair. The movement was so familiar it filled her chest with emotion. He reached behind the counter, lifted the green apron from where it hung, and tied it around his waist with practiced ease.

Ivy made a broken sound in the back of her throat.

Thorn rolled up his sleeves, exposing his forearms. The script was no longer glowing but looked like black tattoos.

"Update," he said evenly, eyes on hers. "Now."

Her lips parted. Closed. Opened again.

"There's..." She swallowed hard. "There's a restaurant. Two hundred centerpieces. Fifty bouquets. They need everything in four hours."

His brows lifted slightly. Not in alarm but in recalibration.

"My rose inventory is almost gone," she rushed on.

"The phone won't stop ringing. There's a line out the door and I haven't even started the restaurant order and I don't know how I'm supposed to do all of this." Her voice broke. "And there's a lot of online orders."

Thorn stepped closer, just enough that she could feel him, solid and real. "Pause," he said.

She looked at him helplessly.

"Breathe," Thorn ordered, softer now.

She did. Once. Twice.

"Good," he said. "I am here."

Something in her finally gave way.

"I'm so glad," she whispered. "I thought I lost you."

"I will not leave you," Thorn said, already reaching for a clipboard. He scanned the top order sheet. His jaw tightened. "Evan?" he asked.

"He's doing deliveries," Ivy said faintly.

"I will handle logistics," Thorn said. "You handle customers."

She shook her head. "The contract?"

He met her gaze. "We will discuss it later."

He slid a bucket closer, already sorting stems with practiced hands. "For now," Thorn continued, "we make flowers."

The phone rang again.

Thorn reached over and answered it without looking. "Calder Floral," he said. "Yes. We can take your order."

Ivy stared at him, heart pounding, disbelief and relief colliding so hard it almost hurt.

She rang up the next customer and noticed that the display shelves were nearly empty. She needed to restock those.

As she greeted the next customer she heard Thorn on the phone with the flower supplier. There was something in his voice she recognized from the day of the break in. He had a certain charm in his efficiency.

"Hey, security is back," Evan shouted as he came in with his empty cart. He made his way to the counter and Ivy handed him the next set of deliveries. "You needed some help," he said. "I've never seen this shop so busy."

Ivy smiled. "Yes." She pointed at the manifest. "I need you to get these delivered and get back as soon as possible. We have a huge order for a restaurant. Over two-hundred and fifty items."

Evan's eyes went wide. "That's amazing!" he congratulated her then looked to Thorn.

Thorn was making a face like he was ready to fight.

"Whoa, calm down security man."

"We don't have time for small talk," Thorn said.

Evan raised his hands in defeat. "Okay. Okay. I'm on it. I'll drive fast and take a lot of chances."

"Don't damage the arrangements," Thorn warned.

Ivy coughed and rubbed her throat as she watched the men banter. She cleared her throat a few times but the ache wouldn't go away. After talking so much this morning, she thought it was worse.

When she looked up, Thorn was watching her.

"I'm fine," Ivy was quick to say.

"You haven't eaten." It wasn't a question.

"There wasn't time."

Something dark flashed in his eyes and Ivy finished ringing out the customers before heading to the cooler to get more arrangements for the shelves.

She saw her breath as she stepped into the cooler. The door closed behind her and she turned, startled.

"You would have not eaten all day if I were here," Thorn accused.

"I don't know. Probably not. It's too busy." She turned to reach for a crate of arrangements but a hand on her arm stopped her.

"Come here," Thorn's voice was low.

She didn't argue. That might have been the most frightening part.

He guided her back a step, away from the shelves, until her back brushed the metal door and no one could see them from the other side of the glass. The cooler hummed around them, cold and sterile and far too quiet for how close he was standing.

"You're shaking," Thorn said.

"I'm cold," she replied automatically.

His gaze sharpened. "You are depleted."

She huffed a weak laugh. "Wow. Thank you, Doctor Demon."

"Ivy," he said, and her name cut through the sarcasm like a blade. "Your throat hurts. Your hands are unsteady. You have not consumed enough calories to sustain this pace. I am disappointed."

She opened her mouth to deny it and stopped when her voice came out rough. "I'll eat later."

"There is no later," Thorn said. "There is now."

He released her arm and his closeness was casual and controlled. It made her stomach flip anyway.

"What are you doing?" she asked, though she already knew.

Thorn lifted his hand between them. He didn't draw a blade. He didn't need one. He used a sharp fang and cut a thin line across his palm.

"I am offering," he said evenly. "Not enforcing. Tell me no and I will stop."

Ivy's breath caught.

Blood in the cooler felt scandalous. Dangerous. Her body reacted before her mind could assemble a sensible objection.

"I shouldn't," she whispered.

"You should," Thorn replied. "Your body requires it. You are changing and now you must."

Her gaze dropped to his palm. The scent hit her, iron and something deeper, threaded with heat that made her pulse stutter.

She swallowed and winced.

Thorn noticed.

"That pain will pass," he said quietly. "If you accept."

Her eyes lifted to his. "Is this..." She hesitated. "Is this the bond?"

"Yes," Thorn said without hesitation.

Something in her chest tightened. "So it's not just... blood."

"No," he said. "It is recognition."

That should have frightened her more than it did.

Ivy reached for his hand with numb fingers and hesitated only a second before pressing her mouth to his skin. The first taste stole her breath. Warmth flooded her throat immediately, spreading downward, easing the ache that had grown sharp and constant. The discomfort faded like it had never existed replaced by a steady, grounding heat throughout her body that made her knees weak.

She took only a little.

Thorn exhaled slowly when she pulled back, jaw tight. He closed his hand, the cut sealing beneath her gaze.

Ivy leaned back against the door, blinking. "That worked."

"Yes."

She touched her throat. "It's gone."

"I know."

She looked at him, searching his face. "You didn't even ask."

"I did not need to," Thorn said. "You were already past refusal."

She snorted softly. "You're terrifying."

"I am attentive," he corrected.

He reached past her, lifted the crate of arrangements like it weighed nothing, and turned toward the door.

"Ivy," Thorn said over his shoulder as he pushed it open, cold air spilling back into the shop. "Do not wait that long again."

She followed him out, still a little dazed. "What if I do?"

He glanced back at her, eyes dark and intent.

"Then I will notice," Thorn said.

And then he was gone into the busy shop again, flowers in hand, leaving Ivy standing in the doorway of the cooler feeling warm, steady, and uncomfortably aware that being cared for like this might be the most dangerous thing of all.

Chapter Twenty-Two

The flower delivery truck arrived just after noon.

Again Ivy heard the low grind of an engine slowing out front and the hiss of air brakes. The back doors opened and buckets upon buckets of flowers filled the sidewalk. Roses wrapped in brown paper. Crates of greenery. Boxes marked with bold Sharpie notes: *RUSH. PRIORITY. HANDLE WITH CARE.*

Ivy looked at Thorn. "You did it," she breathed. "This is a miracle."

Thorn flashed a quick smile, quick and sharp, like he'd allowed himself exactly one second of pride and then he was moving. He lifted crates as if they weighed nothing and carried them inside two at a time, already calling out instructions.

"Roses to the left cooler. Greens straight back. Do not stack the ranunculus. They bruise."

Ivy blinked. "I didn't even say that yet."

"You didn't need to," Thorn replied, already gone.

The shop erupted into motion.

Buckets were cleared, replaced, labeled. Ivy barely had time to react before Thorn was setting stations. The design table was cleared, ribbon sorted, water levels checked. The air filled with the clean, green scent of fresh stems and wet paper.

"Okay," Ivy said, snapping herself into gear. "Okay. We can do this."

They could do this.

Orders flew off the board faster than she could cross them out. Bouquets were stacked neatly by delivery time. Thorn moved through the space like a conductor, voice low and steady, directing chaos into shape.

The bell over the door jingled hard.

Evan stepped in, stamping snow from his boots. "Wow," he said, eyes going wide. "Looks busy."

"Evan," Ivy said sharply, already halfway to the counter. "I need—"

"You," Thorn cut in calmly, turning to face him.

Evan straightened without realizing he was doing it. "Uh. Yeah?"

"You will assist," Thorn said. "Restaurant order. Two hundred centerpieces. Fifty bouquets. Loading and transport."

Evan's mouth fell open. "That's... a lot."

"Yes," Thorn agreed. "You will be careful. You will not rush. You will follow instructions exactly."

Evan glanced at Ivy. She opened her mouth to soften it and stopped when Evan nodded eagerly.

"Absolutely," Evan said. "Yeah. I can do that. I'll grab the dollies."

Thorn handed him a stack of manifests. "In order. By table number. Check them twice. Don't mess this up."

Evan took them with surprising seriousness. "Got it."

He loaded crates without complaint. He asked questions. He triple-checked addresses and names against the orders. When a ribbon spool snapped loose, he fixed it instead of leaving it for someone else. He ran back and forth between the truck and the shop, cheeks flushed from the cold, eyes focused.

Ivy watched him for a second, stunned.

"Is this... happening?" she murmured.

Thorn passed her a bundle of eucalyptus. "Competence is contagious."

She snorted and got back to work.

The hours blurred.

Music played softly from Ivy's phone, something romantic and instrumental, half-buried beneath the rhythm of scissors and the murmur of voices. The shop phone rang constantly, but every call ended in confirmation instead of panic. The line at the counter moved. No one yelled. No one complained.

At one point, Ivy realized she was laughing at an awkward joke from a customer.

She caught Thorn's eye across the shop. He was tying off a bouquet with practiced hands, apron dusted with petals, sleeves rolled, script beneath his skin on display. He met her gaze and something like warmth passed between them. It wasn't the dangerous flare of the bond, but something quieter.

By the time Evan wheeled the last restaurant order

toward the door, sweat-damp and grinning, the shop looked... victorious.

"That's the last of them," Evan said. "Dining room opens in twenty. We're good. I've got plenty of time to get there and unload."

"Thank you," Ivy said, voice thick with disbelief.

Evan scratched the back of his neck. "Hey. I like this place. I'd hate to see it fail." He swiped at his forehead. "It's hot in here."

"Prop the front door open on your way out," Ivy said.

Thorn watched him for a moment, then nodded once. "You performed well."

Evan blinked. "Uh. Thanks?"

He nudged a door stopper into place and let the cool air into the overheated shop.

Ivy leaned against the counter, chest heaving, heart pounding. She looked around. The coolers were full. The order board was cleared. Orders were labeled and stacked. Flowers were everywhere.

She laughed, breathless. "I didn't know a demon could do this," she said, shaking her head, "but you just saved my entire life. And here I had promised you my soul."

Thorn stepped closer, voice low so only she could hear.

"No," he said. "You built this. I simply ensured it did not fall. I am bound to this shop. I am bound to you."

Ivy met his gaze, overwhelmed in a way that had nothing to do with fear.

And for the first time all day, she believed him. Until the sound of shattering glass echoed throughout the shop.

Chapter Twenty-Three

A SHARP CRACK TORE THROUGH THE SHOP, FROM the splintering crash of a display shelf collapsing inward. Ivy flinched, hands flying up instinctively as shards skittered across the floor like thrown ice.

Someone screamed.

It might have been her.

A rock lay in the center of the shop, half-buried beneath broken glass and wilted petals. Snow drifted in through the propped open door, melting instantly against the warmth of the space that had felt so protected just moments ago.

"Not again," Ivy breathed.

Thorn was already moving.

The air around him snapped tight, shadows recoiling then surging as he crossed the shop in a single stride.

A figure bolted down the sidewalk, hood up, shoes slipping on snow.

"Thorn—wait!" Ivy shouted.

The door slammed open hard enough to rattle the hinges.

Cold rushed in as Thorn cleared the threshold and disappeared into the street, moving inhumanly fast.

Ivy stumbled forward, heart hammering. "Thorn!"

Outside, footsteps pounded and a shout cut through the winter air.

Customers pressed back from the counter, murmuring in fear. Someone pulled out a phone. Another person whispered, "What the hell was that?"

Ivy didn't answer.

She ran to the door and stopped short, fingers digging into the frame.

Thorn stood halfway down the block.

The would-be vandal was on the ground, pinned facedown in the snow, Thorn's knee pressed between his shoulder blades.

"Do not," Thorn said, voice low and terrifyingly calm, "move."

The person beneath him sobbed, words tumbling out in panic. "I didn't—I swear—I was just—"

"You threw a stone," Thorn said. "At a protected space."

Ivy's stomach dropped.

She ran.

"Thorn!" she yelled, slipping on the snow as she reached them. "Stop. Don't do this."

Thorn turned his head just enough to see her.

For a split second, the shadows stilled.

The man beneath him was shaking violently now. "Please," he cried. "I'm just a kid."

"Get up," Ivy said sharply, crouching beside Thorn. "Now. Before you make this worse."

Thorn hesitated.

The Ledger beneath his skin flared and it was angry, reactive, *hungry*.

Then Ivy touched his arm.

Bare skin to bare skin.

"Thorn," she said, quieter now. "This is not how we do things."

Something in him shifted like a blade turned away at the last possible moment. He lifted his knee.

The kid scrambled to his feet, slipping on the icy pavement before catching himself against the brick wall.

Ivy's breath left her in a sharp, startled exhale.

"Oh," she whispered. "It's you."

He looked up, wild-eyed and shaking, hoodie torn, hands scraped raw from the fall. It was the same teenager from earlier in the week—the one Thorn had stopped mid-theft. The one Ivy had let go with a warning and a lecture about consequences.

The one who hadn't listened.

"I—I didn't mean—" the kid stammered, words tangling together. "I just—my friends dared me. I didn't think—"

Thorn took one step forward.

The shadows at his feet tightened, coiling like restrained teeth.

"I should have killed him," Thorn said quietly.

The words were not shouted. They didn't need to be.

The kid made a small, terrified sound and pressed himself harder against the wall, hands raised instinctively like that might stop what was coming.

Ivy spun on Thorn. "No."

Her voice cracked through the cold like a whip.

"No," she said again, louder. "You will not say that. You will not *think* that."

"He violated the boundary," Thorn replied, gaze never leaving the boy. "He damaged a protected space. He escalated after mercy. This is a pattern."

"This is a *kid*," Ivy snapped. "A scared, stupid kid who made a bad decision."

"He returned after warning," Thorn said. "In Hell, that is intent. That is punishable by death."

"Well, this isn't Hell," Ivy shot back. She stepped deliberately between them, heart pounding as she put her body in the line Thorn would have taken. "And you don't get to decide who lives."

The Ledger flared beneath his skin, agitated.

The boy slid down the wall, knees giving out completely now. "Please," he sobbed. "Please don't let him kill me."

Ivy didn't look at him. She was watching Thorn.

"You promised," she said quietly. "You said you would control it."

Thorn's jaw flexed. Then he slowly stepped back. The shadows withdrew, snapping inward like they'd been yanked on a leash.

Ivy exhaled shakily and reached into her coat pocket, fingers trembling as she pulled out her phone.

"I'm calling the police," she said, already dialing. "That's how this ends. Not with blood. Not with you destroying yourself."

The kid let out a broken sob of relief and curled in on himself, forehead pressed to his knees.

Thorn turned away, staring down the street, fists clenched so tight his knuckles went white.

"It is inefficient," he muttered.

"I don't care," Ivy replied, voice hoarse. "It's right. This kid," she paused, "what's your name?"

"J—James," the kid's voice was trembling.

"Okay. James still has time to get his life together," Ivy said.

The police arrived within minutes. Two squad cars, lights flashing softly against the snow. The officers took one look at the broken glass, the shaking teenager, Ivy's pale face.

One of them guided the boy upright, hands firm but not rough, while the other produced a pair of cuffs. The metal clicked closed around his wrists, sharp and final in the cold air.

"That's enough," the older officer said, voice edged with weary frustration. "You just can't seem to stay out of trouble, can you?"

The boy flinched, shoulders curling inward. "I didn't think—"

"That's the problem," the officer interrupted. "You don't think. We talked about this last time. We warned you."

Ivy watched his face crumble at the words *last time*. The weight of it pressed into her chest.

The younger officer shook his head. "Breaking windows. Vandalizing a business on the busiest day of the year. You know how bad this could've gone?"

"I'm sorry," the boy whispered, tears streaking down his

face. "I just—everyone said it would be funny after getting in trouble the first time."

"Funny?" the older officer echoed. "You scared people. You cost someone money. You're lucky no one got hurt. You need to hang out with better friends."

The officer glanced toward Ivy, then back to the boy. "You don't get many more chances like this. You hear me?"

The boy nodded frantically, hands trembling in the cuffs. "Yes, sir."

"Good," the officer said. "Because next time, it won't be a warning."

They guided him toward the patrol car, one hand steady on his shoulder as they walked.

As they led him away, the kid looked back once, eyes red and terrified.

"I'm sorry," he whispered.

Ivy nodded once. "I know."

The car doors closed. The engines started. The street went quiet again.

Thorn finally turned back to her.

"You will continue to choose mercy," he said.

"Yes," Ivy replied. "Every time."

Chapter Twenty-Four

Ivy stood there for a moment too long, staring at the patch of disturbed snow where the boy had been, her breath coming shallow and uneven. The cold finally reached her, sharp and biting, slipping beneath her coat like it had been waiting its turn.

Her hands started to shake.

"Hey," Thorn said softly.

She tried to answer him and failed. Her knees felt loose, disconnected.

"I'm fine," she said automatically.

Thorn did not accept that.

He stepped in close, careful not to crowd her, and rested a steadying hand at her elbow. The warmth of him bled through her coat, grounding in a way that made her eyes burn.

"You are not," he said. "Your adrenaline has surged. Your body is protesting."

She huffed out something that might have been a laugh. "Wow. You make it sound very dramatic."

"It is," Thorn replied.

Her legs wobbled again and this time she didn't fight it when he guided her back toward the shop. The door was still propped open.

A customer had started cleaning up the broken glass.

"We'll get that," Ivy waved them away. "You don't have to do that."

"We help our own," the woman said and Ivy recognized her from the shop down the street.

"Thank you."

Ivy leaned against the counter, suddenly exhausted down to her bones. Thorn helped clean up the broken shelf then he closed the shop door.

They worked in silence for a while. Not the frantic rush of earlier, but the deliberate, end-of-day kind. Thorn swept. Ivy wiped down the counter. He re-tied ribbons that had been rushed earlier, straightened cards, checked delivery tags. She wrapped the final bouquets with care.

When the last order was placed in its crate and the lights were dimmed to evening glow, Ivy set her shears down and exhaled long and slow.

"That's it," she said. "That's everything. I can barely believe we got all of this done. I will never be able to thank you enough."

Thorn turned the sign to *Closed*.

Then he looked at her. "You are going upstairs," he said.

She blinked. "I am?"

"Yes," Thorn said. "You will change your clothes."

Her brow furrowed. "Why?"

"Because," he said, voice gentler now, "you deserve to be seen tonight as more than someone who worked herself to exhaustion. You have never had time to go out to dinner. Tonight you will."

Her throat tightened unexpectedly.

"What are you planning?" she asked.

"You will see," Thorn replied.

He pressed a warm hand briefly to her lower back, guiding her toward the stairs before she could overthink it. "Go."

Ivy stood in front of her closet longer than necessary. She reached past the familiar work clothes and paused. Her fingers brushed fabric she hadn't worn in over a year.

A simple dress in deep red, not flashy but classic in its design. A square neck and elbow length sleeves. She'd bought it for a dinner that never happened. For a life she'd assumed she'd get back to someday.

She changed slowly, smoothing the fabric over her hips, twisting her hair down from its bun and letting it fall loose. She washed her face, added a touch of color to her cheeks and her lips. When she looked in the mirror again, she barely recognized herself. Her heart beat a little faster as she stepped back into the hallway.

Downstairs, the shop lights glowed warm and low. And whatever Thorn had planned, she sensed it wasn't about flowers. It was about *her*.

Ivy stood at the top of the stairs and heard Thorn and

Evan's voices as they got the last of the orders out the door. When she heard the lock click, she started down the stairs.

The shop was quiet—no phones ringing, no bell chiming, no footsteps outside. Just the low hum of the coolers.

Thorn stood behind the counter.

The Ledger lay open in front of him.

Ivy stopped short.

It was not the crisp, innocuous-looking contract she remembered signing. The paper looked heavier now, darker at the edges, the ink no longer flat black but threaded through with a deep, rusted red. The words shifted subtly when she looked away and back again, like they were still deciding her fate.

"Why do you have that?" she asked quietly.

"I must make a decision," Thorn replied.

She approached slowly.

Thorn rested both palms on the counter, shoulders squared. This wasn't the Thorn who'd hauled crates or tied ribbons or made her coffee. This was the demon who enforced contracts. The weapon Hell had forged.

"Ledger Demons exist to collect," he said. "We are violent by necessity. We enforce consequence. We remove choice."

Ivy swallowed. "I don't like those rules."

"I know."

She met his gaze. "I don't believe in death as punishment. I don't believe in terror as motivation. And I don't believe anyone should lose their soul because they were desperate."

The Ledger pulsed faintly.

Thorn nodded once. "That is precisely why this cannot continue."

Her heart started to race. "What do you mean?"

"Being a Ledger Demon requires compliance," Thorn said. "Compliance requires collectability. As long as I exist within the Ledger's system, Hell can reclaim me. Hell could claim you if it wanted to."

"And if they reclaim you?" Ivy asked.

"Then I am erased," Thorn finished. "Or you are."

She shook her head. "No. There has to be another way."

"There is," Thorn said.

The way he said it frightened her.

"I have been evaluating the structure," he continued. "The Ledger feeds on ownership. On classification. On enforceable identity."

He gestured to the contract. The words on the page rippled.

"I cannot void it from within," Thorn said. "But I can make myself uncollectible."

Ivy frowned. "How?"

Thorn looked at her. "By binding myself," he said, "to something Hell cannot lawfully claim."

Her pulse thundered. "Something like...?"

"You."

The word landed heavy.

Ivy's breath left her in a rush. "Thorn... What does that mean?"

"Ivy," he interrupted gently. "You already carry the beginning of the bond."

She touched her throat. Heat bloomed there in quiet recognition.

"The blood bond initiated a transfer of priority," Thorn said. "The Ledger recognizes it. It is attempting to reassert dominance."

He turned the book toward her.

"Read."

Her hands trembled as she leaned over the counter.

The text was no longer the same.

IN EXCHANGE FOR RELIEF FROM BURDENS OF THE *business Calder Floral, the undersigned offers—*

THE WORDS STRUCK THROUGH THEMSELVES.

New script threaded beneath it.

IN EXCHANGE FOR SEVERANCE FROM THE LEDGER, *the undersigned offers binding of self to Ivy Calder. This bond supersedes all claims. This bond is entered willingly. This bond is irreversible.*

IVY'S VISION BLURRED.

"This isn't what I signed," she whispered.

"No," Thorn agreed. "It is what I am signing."

Her heart slammed against her ribs. "You're talking about ending Ledger Demons."

"Yes."

She looked up sharply. "All of them?"

"If I succeed," Thorn said, "the classification fractures. Enforcement collapses. Others may follow."

"And Hell?" she asked.

"Hell loses a weapon. But we are an old construct from lifetimes before. The new Queen has changed much. I don't think they will be upset about it." Thorn said calmly.

Ivy stared at him, horror and awe tangling together. "You're dismantling an entire system."

Her voice shook. "You'd do this for me?"

He stepped closer, the warmth of him undeniable now. "I would do this because of you."

She pressed her palm flat against the page, feeling the thrum beneath it. "And me?"

"You are protected," Thorn said. "Bound by choice, not threat."

Ivy laughed once, breathless and terrified. "You're really doing this."

"Yes." She met his gaze, searching for hesitation but there was none.

"Okay," she said quietly.

The Ledger pulsed violently, ink crawling like veins. Thorn placed his hand over hers on the page.

The pages shuddered violently, the paper flexing like skin pulled too tight over bone. The shop lights flickered. Somewhere deep beneath the floorboards, something answered.

Ivy sucked in a breath. "It knows."

"Yes," Thorn said. "And it objects."

The ink began to rewrite itself without either of them touching it, letters scoring themselves into the page.

"This must be spoken," he said. "Not written."

Her pulse roared in her ears. "What do I have to say?"

"Nothing," Thorn replied. "This is my severance."

The temperature in the shop plummeted. Thorn drew the small knife from his coat pocket. He turned it once in his hand, testing the weight.

Ivy's breath hitched. "Thorn—"

"If you stop me," he said quietly, "the Ledger will retain claim."

Her hands clenched into fists. "I won't."

Thorn pressed the blade to his palm and cut deep. Blood welled immediately He let it fall. The first drop struck the paper.

"By blood unclaimed," he said, voice steady, deliberate, "I revoke classification."

Script burned through the cover, glowing red-hot as words tried to assert themselves.

LEDGER   DEMON.   ENFORCEMENT   ASSET. Property of

THORN SPOKE OVER IT.

"The unbound," he continued, "I reject collection. By choice," Thorn said, louder now, "I sever myself from all registries."

The text changed again.

Her name appeared first, written in steady ink.

Ivy Calder

Below it, Thorn's name followed. No demon classification. No ledger seal.

Only a final line, burning itself into existence one letter at a time.

Thorn bound by choice. Uncollectable.

The page burst into flame.

Thorn gasped.

He dropped to one knee as the script beneath his skin ignited, lines tearing themselves loose from his body like hooks ripping free. He cried out once as the marks seared his skin in permanent tattoo, leaving behind proof of what they'd done.

Bound by choice. Uncollectable.

The phrase repeated over and over again across his skin.

Ivy stared at the paper she'd signed nearly a week ago, then at Thorn. "Did it work?"

He closed his eyes briefly, testing something inside himself and reaching for power that no longer answered the same way.

"Yes," he said. "I am... uncollectable."

Relief hit her so hard she nearly sobbed.

Then Thorn stiffened.

A DEMON HAD REWRITTEN HIMSELF AFTER HE FELL in love with one mortal woman.

Chapter Twenty-Five

Ivy had been waiting for Thorn to come back; he had gone up to the apartment to change. He came down the stairs nearly running and wearing a dark jacket, crisp shirt, sleeves rolled the way she liked. He looked... handsome.

"Hi," she said softly.

Thorn's gaze traced her like he was cataloging proof that this was real. "I forgot to tell you earlier, you look... remarkable, Ivy."

Her mouth curved into a smile that felt unfamiliar. Lighter. "You clean up well yourself."

He opened the door for her.

Outside, the night was cold and clear. The city hummed softly, unaware of what had almost been lost on this day.

Thorn offered his arm.

She took it.

The walk was just two blocks and then Thorn pointed

to a building. The restaurant ahead was bright and festive, its windows glowing gold against the dark. The same place that had nearly broken her that morning. The same place she'd saved.

Ivy slowed.

"No," she breathed. "You didn't."

"I did," Thorn said. "They insisted. Said they wanted to thank the florist personally."

Her chest tightened. "Thorn, this place is ridiculously expensive."

"I know," he replied gently. "Do not consider price."

Inside, the space was transformed.

Every table bore their work. There were low arrangements of roses and greens, candlelight woven through stems and petals. The dining room felt alive, warm, humming with celebration. Laughter filled the air. Glasses clinked. Life continued.

The owner, Don, spotted her immediately.

"There she is!" he exclaimed, hurrying over. "Ivy Calder. You saved my Valentine's Day. This—" He gestured wildly at the room. "—this would not exist without you."

Ivy flushed, overwhelmed. "I'm just glad it worked out."

"It did more than work," he said warmly. "The guests are very happy. Dinner is on us. Tonight and always. You've got a standing table here."

She laughed softly, dazed, and let Thorn guide her to their seat.

They sat near the window.

For a while, neither of them spoke.

Ivy watched the room. The people. The gestures to the flowers.

"I've never done this," she said finally.

"Dinner?" Thorn asked.

"Celebrating," she replied. "Celebrating the shop. It's been a rough eight years hoping every year I'd get by."

His gaze softened. "You should have been allowed to do this long ago."

She looked at him.

"You're still here," she said quietly.

"Yes."

"And they didn't take you."

"No."

"And the shop…"

"Safe."

Her throat tightened. "I don't know what tomorrow looks like."

Thorn reached across the table and took her hand. His touch was warm.

"Neither do I," he said. "But it will be ours."

Food arrived. Wine. Something decadent she would normally never order.

Ivy laughed when she realized she wasn't rushing. Wasn't counting minutes. Wasn't thinking about what she had to do next.

For the first time in years, Valentine's Day had given her something back.

Later, when they stepped back out into the cold, Ivy paused on the sidewalk, breath fogging the air.

"Thank you," she said. "For everything."

Thorn considered her carefully.

"I was created to collect," he said. "Tonight, I am simply... grateful."

She smiled up at him, slipping her hand into his.

Epilogue

One Year Later

The bell over the door chimed at exactly eight.

Ivy smiled to herself as she flipped the sign from *Closed* to *Open* and let the first wave of Valentine's Day customers spill inside. Snow clung to coats and boots. Breath fogged the air. Love notes were clutched in nervous hands.

Calder Floral was warm, the kind of warmth that came from people who knew the space would hold.

The shop had changed in a year. New shelving. A larger cooler. A second design table along the east wall where sunlight hit in the morning. A small brass plaque near the register read:

. . .

Established by choice.

Most customers didn't notice it.

The ones who mattered always asked but it only got them to witness Ivy and Thorn glancing at each other and Ivy blushing.

"I can't believe how calm it feels in here," a woman murmured as Ivy rang her up. "It's Valentine's Day and I don't feel like screaming."

Ivy laughed softly. "We specialize in that."

Behind her, Thorn adjusted a bouquet with steady hands. His apron was red now and he wore a dark button-down, sleeves rolled, hair tied back at the nape of his neck. He still moved with that same precise grace, but there was nothing sharp about it now.

A year ago, this day had nearly broken them.

"Delivery schedule's tight but manageable," Thorn said quietly, handing Ivy a clipboard. "Restaurant order is confirmed. Evan's already loading."

"Of course he is," Ivy said fondly.

The bell chimed again.

Someone paused just inside the door, hesitant. Ivy glanced up and felt her chest tighten.

The teenager from last year stood there—taller now, hands shoved deep into his jacket pockets. His gaze flicked to the repaired window, then to the floor.

"I—I just wanted to say," he started, voice awkward. "I'm... I'm working at the hardware store now. Mr. Larkin hired me." He swallowed. "I'm sorry. For everything." He picked up a bouquet of a dozen pink roses and brought them to the counter.

Ivy didn't look at Thorn. She could feel him watching.

She smiled. "Thank you for saying that." Ivy rang up the bouquet. "Who are these for?"

The boy nodded quickly, relief written all over him. "They're for my mother. No one has ever given her flowers before. I saved up all year."

"She will love these," Ivy promised. "Thank you for coming back."

Thorn watched the door close, then turned to her. "You were right."

"I know," Ivy said.

Around noon, the rush softened. Orders thinned. The shop settled into a steady hum.

Ivy leaned against the counter, exhaling. "I used to dread this day."

"You no longer do," Thorn said.

"No," she admitted. "Now I just... work. And then I go to dinner."

His mouth curved. "Speaking of."

She glanced at the clock. "Already?"

"Time is cooperative when no one owns you," he replied.

They locked up just after seven.

Outside, the city glowed. Couples laughed. Someone nearby argued over directions. Life continued—messy, ordinary, unremarkable in the way that meant everything had held.

At the restaurant, the owner greeted them, old friends now.

"To the florist who saved my business," he declared, raising a glass. "To a year of beautiful flowers all over this restaurant."

Ivy flushed.

Thorn simply inclined his head, unbothered by the attention. He no longer carried the weight of systems on his shoulders. No enforcement. No collection.

Only presence.

Later, walking home through softly falling snow, Ivy slipped her hand into his.

"You ever regret it?" she asked quietly. "Leaving Hell?"

Thorn considered the question, hand drifting to his neck and the letters etched into the skin.

"No," he said. "I regret that I was made to believe I did not have a choice sooner. I regret that I hesitated. I will never regret that life because it led me to you."

She squeezed his hand.

At the top of the stairs, before unlocking the door, he paused.

"One year," Thorn said. "No summons. No registry. No claim."

Ivy smiled up at him. "Sounds like freedom."

"Yes," he agreed. "And something better."

Inside, the shop lights glowed dim and golden below

them. Flowers waited for tomorrow. For spring. For whatever came next.

For the first time in her life, Ivy didn't wonder how long it would last.

She already knew.

-The End-

Bound by choice. Uncollectable.

A NOTE

Thank You

To every reader who picked up *Ruin has Sharp Fangs*—whether you've been with me since the first Veil of Shadows book or jumped in at The Sky is Starless or you just stumbled across my work on TikTok at 2 a.m. THANK YOU! If this is your first Veil of Shadows book, welcome in! Welcome home. Welcome to the family. We are glad to have you.

You are the reason this world keeps growing. Every like, share, review, and late-night DM fuels my dark little writer heart. And I love responding with: "I wonder what's going to happen next?!"

To my incredible BookTok family: Mellystarr, massiel reads, ShadowDaddy/D, Linda, Kim.d.f.reads, Tameka, Tracy, Cass Marie, Shania, littlekick, sweetpea26_26, Del (I'm still thinking about that alpha rescue, after all this time, nearly every day!), thatgalbritt, punkachoo, Short-.n.sweet, Shannon, curious_kitten, momma Deb, SarLitten, Raye, Platinum_VERA, OkayLucy, DivaSoldierFoster, jennifer7746, Whit, Brianne, Mikayla, Brandi B, Ken, Like.A.Diamond, Mystery Book Bundles, Sam/Dillon, DeyaReads, Jessica, Oopsiedaisies, Sarah, Letty, Chantel, Megs, Mama Guti, Bookinit, AuthorAnnette S, Patty.M.G, Ivan.n.honey, Janet Marie Freels, Andrea, White Booktok, and sooooo many more!! You all make promoting vampires, morally gray MMCs, and slow-burn romance a joy.

To my ARC readers on Booksirens: Thank you, thank you. I love getting your first reviews and thoughts. I love seeing your insta posts and tiktok reviews.

To my editors, Kristy & Massiel: you catch the things I miss and all those extra commas, sharpen every sentence, and saved my deadlines for the new year. I am forever grateful!

To my family: you've listened to my rambling lore dumps, tolerated my writing marathons, my Livestreams, and never once questioned why I'm Googling things like "can you sell your soul to pay the bills?" You're my safe place and my chaos crew, and I love you.

Here's to more books, more worlds, and more late nights. I have many books planned for this year. Let's see if I can write them all!

Tiktok fam, I'm still smiling about the nights you all got me to 1 million likes during the many livestreams in 2025!

2026 is going to be amazing!

Let the Vampires Bite,
    Meredith
    (PS: Melly, it's not a cliffhanger.)

About the Author

M. R. Pritchard delves into the profound clash between good and evil, the mystical realms of gods and monsters, and the intricate transformations of ordinary people into beings of immense power. Her gripping narratives often unfold within the haunting backdrop of apocalyptic or post-apocalyptic landscapes, offering a unique blend of suspense and wonder.

M. R. Pritchard is a two-time Kindle Scout winning author, her short story "Glitch" has been featured in the 2017 winter edition of THE FIRST LINE literary journal. Her short story "Moon Lord" has been featured in Chronicle Worlds: Half Way Home (Part of the Future Chronicles) and will be time capsuled on the moon on the Lunar Codex in 2024.

Visit her website MRPritchard.com and Subscribe. You'll get subscriber only content, deleted scenes, updates, special previews of new projects, and book deals.

Looking to buy direct? Visit MidnightLedgerbooks (dot) com to get signed books, early releases, and extras.